T0129134

THE PHIGON CHRONICLES

The Burning Star

GABRIEL SILVER

authorHOUSE®

AuthorHouse™
1663 Liberty Drive
Bloomington, IN 47403
www.authorhouse.com
Phone: 1 (800) 839-8640

Published by AuthorHouse 06/06/2017

ISBN: 978-1-5246-9116-5 (sc)
ISBN: 978-1-5246-9115-8 (e)

Print information available on the last page.

Any people depicted in stock imagery provided by Thinkstock are models,
and such images are being used for illustrative purposes only.
Certain stock imagery © Thinkstock.

This book is printed on acid-free paper.

Because of the dynamic nature of the Internet, any web addresses or
links contained in this book may have changed since publication and
may no longer be valid. The views expressed in this work are solely those
of the author and do not necessarily reflect the views of the publisher,
and the publisher hereby disclaims any responsibility for them.

CHAPTER 1

HISTORY REPEATS

T HE ATLANTIC NATION, home to the dragons; rulers of the oceanic creatures.

The Air Pyramids home to the Arians, rulers of the sky.

The mystic forest, Fairold home to the fairies, rulers of Spascic's nature and creatures,

Then there is the Volcanic Tribe, home of the flaming bird, the phoenixes.

Dragons and Phoenixes took the forms of humans, but can shift into their beasts.

Fairies looked as if they were abnormal humans. Their ears are pointy, their hair glisten in the sun and sparkled in the night and their hair, when blown in the wind, fluttered glitter dust in the air.

Arians were said to be the earth's angels. They once lived on earth as Greeks and Egyptians. Airians have giant white wings on their backs. People worshipped them as Gods.

A war broke out on earth against these four species, when the humans started hunting and killing them to sell. Many lives were taken. The Airians thought the war had gone far enough and asked the Gods Lalunas and Solajark for guidance and help. The Gods told them that the fairies would need to create a new world from a star, secure enough for them to live. Once the spell was complete the four species fled to this world and created the four nations.

Lalunas said in order for there to be balance and stability, there would need to be a king. The fight that will signify who has the power and wisdom to rule all four Kingdoms. Each nation will pick a leader to represent them in the battle called the Andromeda, which will take place every 10 years.

The last ruler was a Phoenix. The most powerful and ruthless in all the history of rulers. He possessed the power of blue fire, a forbidden technique, resulting in him gaining the title as King of Spascic.

His name was Wetchador. Dictating and conquering, Wetchador wanted everyone to be like a Phoenix; burning with passion and driven to have power.

His goals were for everyone to look alike, dress alike, and move alike. He wanted to expand the Volcanic Tribes way of living. Spreading the life of a Phoenix to all the kingdoms.

Wetchador was hungry for more territory. He set out to take over more land. His first destination was the

Air Pyramids. In his eyes, the Airians were insult to the Gods. Their way of living free was a cancer to his land. Their minds were weak. So weak that he knew there was no challenge there. The Pegasus riders are very free spirited and peaceful minded people. They do not participate in chaotic behavior, they save their energy for the Andromeda. So, they put up no fight when Wetchador raided their nation.

The Atlantic Nation were no pushovers. The dragons went to war against the Phoenixes to defend their territory. The war lasted for almost a century. But due to their losses in battle, they did not want to sacrifice more lives and decided to let Wetchador have his time as king, knowing that his reign will come to an end soon.

Wetchador was on a winning streak. His last destination was Fairold. Saving the best for last, he was going to take pride in raiding this nation. They were casted as witches on Earth, and Wetchador still saw them as that. Demons who plagued the world they lived in.

His view of the fairies blinded him to what he was walking into. He underestimated them.

Wetchador went to the leader of the fairies Myrtle Merlow; who represented them in the last Andromeda. He presented his ideas of a new world to her. But she didn't see that as the way of the fairies. Myrtle turned down his offer, preparing for him to launch another war.

Wetchador was always one step ahead. Instead of taking their kingdom by force, he decided to teach a lesson to Myrtle.He held a festival, honoring the Fairies for their independence in the world. Myrtle attended as the guest of honor along with her son Fritel.

Wetchador watched as the festival played out. After a few hours he spoke. Making a toast, he rose up with his Phoenix sword made of black steel. Streaks of magma made the sword glow in the air. He shot a burst of flame from his mouth, silencing everyone. Wetchador spoke of how proud he was to be the king. He went on to say the fairies did not want to merge the nations together.

He noticed that Myrtle had brought her son. They were standing in the center of the crowd. He asked Fritel to come stand next to him to help give respect to his mother's honor.

Myrtle was hesitant, she knew something was not right. She tried to talk pull Fritel back but he continued to walk assuring his mother that everything was fine.

"Today is the day where we honor the Fairies' independence..." he shouted, wrapping his arm around Fritel. "They decided to not join me on my journey in making Spascic great again," he said as the Phoenixes cheered him on.

He was absorbing all of the attention.

Wetchador turned to Fritel. "But no matter, this kingdom will still rise." Wetchador raised his sword and the crowd cheered him on.

"I want to give a gift to the Fairies and their leader Ms. Myrtle Merlow, who actually had the opportunity to fight me in the Andromeda," Wetchador said confidently.

He walked behind Fritel and put both his hands on his shoulders. He leaned in to whisper to him, "Thank your mother."

Wetchador ripped through Fritel's chest, plunging through his body, searching for his heart. Myrtle tried to run up to save him, but was held back by two guards. Pulling out his heart, Wetchador tossed Fritel to the ground like a rag doll.

The crowd abruptly went silent.

Myrtle immediately screamed "attack!" issuing for a war to start. Her eyes filled up with tears as they reflected the flames Wetchador conjured up from his hands to burn the heart of her son to ashes. She looked Wetchador in the eyes, noticing he was wearing a devilish smirk on his face, as he blew the ashes at her, giving her a wink.

In an instant, Myrtle teleported towards Wetchador gripping his neck, stabbing her long, sharp purple nails into his skin. "You will rue this day!" she growled. "I will make you regret your life after this!" She pushed him back releasing him from her grasp. He never broke eye contact with her, and the smirk never left his face.

Myrtle then turned away. Her long red hair whipped in the wind fluttering glitter. A whistle rang in the crowd, retreating the fairies from fighting, and they teleported back into the forest.

A few months had passed and Wetchador had gave up on waiting for Myrtle's retaliation.

For her, it was just the beginning. She decided to cast a spell on his tribe forcing the Phoenixes to fall in love with the dragons. This created a new and more powerful beast, a Phigon, a mixed breed of the Phoenix and Dragon who possesses unimaginable power that none have ever seen.

Myrtle wanted this new creature to emerge, proving to Wetchador that he will no longer be the most powerful creature in Spascic. The Phigon will be his new threat.

Over time, more and more Phigons were being born. Each Phigon was possessing a power of the elements.

Wetchador could sense the power of these new creatures but didn't feel threatened. He knew that they wouldn't last in combat with him or his army.

Myrtle was not finished with him yet. She then went to the Atlantic Nation, to the most powerful leader of the nation, the woman who almost defeated Wetchador in the Andromeda, Flocean. She had remarkable strength and power. Myrtle knows everything about a person as a fairy. She knew that Flocean didn't have the gift to have children. So Myrtle promised to give her children, if she helped kill Wetchador. She wanted Flocean to make Wetchador fall in love with her. Then rip his heart out, literally.

Flocean hated Wetchador for what he did to the Atlantic Nation. So it would be great to get back at him. Unfortunately for Myrtle, things took a turn. Flocean fell in love with Wetchador, and because Flocean had the gift of birth, she got pregnant with twins boys by Wetchador. When Myrtle found this out, she wanted to kill the king's unborn twins to avenge her own son's death.

On a night of a full moon, the Fairies' powers are heightened. Myrtle snuck into the bedroom where both Wetchador and Flocean were sleeping. Myrtle laid her hands onto Flocean's belly, and sensed an incredible amount of power coming from the twins. Myrtle was ecstatic. The twins were going to be her weapon.

Flocean turned over and was still half asleep. Her eyes cracked open, she saw Myrtle starring at her stomach, with a demonic smile. Flocean gasped. Myrtle shot back and quickly teleported.

Years later the twins were born and had been developing more of their ability. Wetchador had noticed that their power was growing rapidly. He was becoming jealous, threatened by his new sons.

The youngest twin had the power of ice. He was able to sculpt ice and snow into anything using his mind. But he was the only one who could wield his creations.

It was too cold for any other to touch. It was like dry ice that burnt the skin.

The oldest had the power of lightning. When he was a child, crying would cause thunderstorms to emerge. He was able to shoot lightning from his hands. If lightning struck he was able to redirect it into the sky.

When they were 12, they were challenged to fight each other. Whomever won would represent the Volcanic Tribe in the next Andromeda.

Their battle lasted for hours, neither wanted to hurt one another. They danced around dodging each other's attack. But one had to be the victor. The Ice Phigon had always felt close with his father. He related so much with him. He was a prodigy of his father. He wanted to be the next king.

The Lightning Phigon had no desire to be a ruler. He was very attached to his mother. Just like Flocean, he went with the flow of things. He was calm like a lake but knew that he could erupt like a storm at sea. So he tended to stay away from altercations. But there was no running, he was forced to fight.

Blinded by his jealousy, Wetchador couldn't let his sons become more powerful than he was. Witnessing his sons' battle, he realized that he had a new threat. So Wetchador ordered every single Phigon alive be killed.

An army of Phoenixes called Subjeckies demolished the cities, raiding homes and slaughtering every Phigon they had seen. Families hiding their babies were killed. Mothers would commit suicide after watching their babies be murdered.

Flocean tried to hide the twins. She sent for Myrtle to help her, after 12 years.

Myrtle had devised a plan to hide the twins. But before she could hide them, the Lightning Phigon had vanished without a trace. Flocean went out to search for him, but was hung at dawn for treason. The Ice Phigon was hiding in the cellar. Myrtle had made it to the castle of the Phoenix king, just in time to rescue the remaining son. Myrtle took him to safety.

The Subjeckies reported to Wetchador and told him they got rid of any remaining Phigons.

Wetchador asked if they had found his last twin son, but they said there was no trace of either him nor Myrtle. She had disappeared along with the boy.

Several years after Myrtle vanishing, Wetchador conquered the mystic forest. Reining over the world of Spascic, he changed it to the world he set it out to be. One hundred years later after the rule of Wetchador, there was the Next Andromeda, allowing the Air Pyramids to gain control and restoring the nations to their rightful ways and allowing peace to flood the world again.

The new ruler of Atlantic Nation was a young man named Baggasin, and he was very powerful. He studied the techniques that Flocean and past leaders had practiced. Ithilia, a new ruler of the Volcanic Tribe, learned her techniques from her ancestors and mentors and now had the title of the most powerful Phoenix of the generation. When these two met during the Andromeda, they fell in love. With Myrtle's disappearance, the spell was never lifted. After a decade, four new phigons were born.

Salomne, the oldest of all, has the power of the Air element. Grastem the second oldest, has the Earth element. Myosin, the only girl, has the fire ability. Rozel, the youngest, is gifted with the water element.

CHAPTER 2

THE DREAM

ROZEL HAD BEEN having a recurring dream. It haunted him almost every night: Rozel is running through a cave chasing a mysterious man who haunts his dreams. A shining light sneaks in at the end of the cave, silhouetting the running man, but it is hard for Rozel to see. Icy shards hang from the roof of the cave. Rozel can only see his hair, curly, long, and black with a hint of white streaks. It tends to bounce as he runs. His skin is brown, and he is a tall man which makes his movement a bit stiff.

He is running toward the light at the end of the cave, leaving frost puddles with each step. Fog forms from his breath, and glides through the air. It's so cold here.

Distracted by the thought of frostbite, Rozel feels that he might pass out from the cold. But, his prey seems fine.

The man finally makes it out the cave, Rozel right behind him. Not sure if the man notices him, he keeps his distance.

A crunch vibration rings in Rozel's ear when the mystery man takes a step into snow. He then begins to walk towards a form in the distance.Rozel doesn't move, he feels more secure hidden in the shadow of this cave. It's hard to see, the ground is covered in pure white snow. The trees are heavy with it. The sun reflects off the snow and Rozel must squint to make out the form. Leaning any further will make him lose his balance and fall, so he puts his left hand on the wall next to him, covered in ice, hoping it will stabilize his balance. His palm sizzles, burning as if his hand contacted a hot stove.

Immediately snatching his hand back and nursing it with his other hand he bites his lip to hold in the scream. Panting, squeezing his wrist hoping the pain would stop, it instead grew. Never feeling this much pain Rozel's body begins regenerating itself. His water ability allows him to heal himself.

While being burned from the ice, Rozel senses power from the ice, a mystic power. It isn't natural ice. He looks up from his hand and notices the guy kneeling and talking to the tombstone formed from the snow.

To get a look, Rozel tries to lean forward once again. Just before he can react to what he sees, Rozel begins to feel himself losing balance and slowly fall down into the snow. The vibration roams his body and roars in his ears when he hears the sound of the crunch and crackle of the hard snow. Knowing his presence is revealed, Rozel gets up and looks at the mysterious man hoping he didn't see him. But he did.

The man's head sharply whips in the direction of Rozel. He is staring into his soul with a disturbing glare. The man begins to move his arms in a circular motion, similar to the technique Rozel and his brother's practice.

A gust of icy wind is conjured up, surrounding him and the tombstone. Soon after, the gust disappears and along with it was the man and the tombstone.

Whispers appear from the distance, formulating Rozel's name in the wind. He begins to feel the ground shake. "Not again," he mutters.

He wakes up and starts to breathe heavily. Salomne is standing over him, shaking him awake.

Salomne does this often when Rozel has a dream like this. It's been going on for years. Rozel looks up at Salomne showing annoyance in his expression. Whenever Rozel gets close to finding out whom this man might be, Salomne's shaking him awake.

Salomne is the eldest brother and is known for his power to control the element air. He is 22, his eyes are grey like the clouds in the sky. Salomne's hair is dark grey and cut short with the typical gel spike hair on the top of his head. He stands about 6'1 and has a muscular body from his frequent training.

Rozel lifts his head up past Salomne and looks between his curtains out the window. The night was still young. Rozel's room is located in the western part of the castle. As dark as it is, a light from the Burning Star in the sky usually brightens up the room. When he was younger it would shine bright, flickering, as if it was a light bulb. Rozel would stay up all night until dawn. It was a beautiful sight to see. Every time he had a lucid dream similar to the one he just woke up from, he would wake up and see the Burning Star shine bright and then dim fading away in the night sky. Rozel felt a connection to it. But soon after so many nights of waking up and seeing a recurring thing, he began to feel like, perhaps, that was just how the star burns.

CHAPTER 3

I T'S THE NEXT morning and Salomne couldn't sleep. Worried about his younger brother, Salomne didn't know what to do about his brother's dreams.

When Salomne was younger, he had dreams that would become true. As he got older, the dreams soon stopped. Myosin and Grastem had gone through the same predicament, but they were never as surreal as Rozel's.

Now Rozel has been having recurring dream for years, and fear is taking a toll on Salomne. He fears that this may mean something, whether bad or good, something is coming.

With Rozel being the youngest, he is very gullible and naive. He can easily be persuaded to believe that these dreams are a positive. Rozel is known to be easily manipulated by his dreams, so Salomne makes it a priority to watch over him.

Salomne promised to keep this a secret from their parents and the brothers, but he is beginning to feel that this may be bigger than Rozel and himself.

Luckily Salomne sensed Myosin's presence outside of Rozel's room. He overheard the conversation between Salomne and Rozel's dreams.

Salomne and Myosin's relationship has always been rocky ever since Myosin burned Rozel practicing playing with her fire bending. Ever since then, everything has changed between them.

Prying is one of many unloving tendencies Myosin loves to do.

It wouldn't be surprised if this information gets out about Rozel's dreams to their mother and father. In fact, Salomne would be a relieved if she did tell them. Being very big on his promises, it wouldn't be bad if Myosin told them rather than him. It may actually be the only good thing she has done. But unfortunately, knowing Myosin, Salomne knows that if he sensed Myosin out in the halls, it is because she wanted him to.

It was time for training to start and they all started to heading outside in the garden. They stand in a line, side by side, oldest to youngest. Salomne being the oldest is in line first, Grastem is next to him, Myosin follows up and last is Rozel. Bernard, their mentor and their father's best friend, wants to talk to them before they start their training. Grastem notices that Bernard has a worried look on his face.

Bernard begins to speak, and he is saying their focus needs to be keen. The Andromeda is three years from now. That will be the time where they must battle one another. Due to each one of them being the most powerful creatures and having an elemental ability. The previous leaders, who represented the nations in the last Andromeda, decided that the best chance at their nation winning the next Andromeda would be to let the phigons fight for them. With their power being limitless, the phigons would not only put on an amazing performance, but any one of them would make great leaders and rulers. Salomne would represent the Air Pyramids nation, Grastem would represent Fairold, Myosin is representing the Volcanic Tribe and Rozel is representing the Atlantic Nation.

Bernard is speaking of this as if it was their first time hearing of this. But they learned of this long ago.

Grastem has always believed that Salomne would be the new ruler, due to him having better control over his power. But Myosin also has a chance. Having the ability of fire, means she has the advantage over Grastem.

Myosin looks at herself as the black sheep. When she didn't have a handle on her power, she burned everything she touched; Salomne once had scrolls written by ancient ancestors brought from other worlds, given to him by the Fairies. Unintentionally, Myosin burned them to ashes, before he had the chance to read them.

After a while she began to distance herself, and soon became rebellious. She assumed no one wanted to be around her. She had to become her own entertainment. She played jokes on her brothers; Grastem would practice creating flowers from the ground. Myosin would come over and say, "Oh, how beautiful. May I hold it?" her sarcasm was obvious. She held it then burned it to ash.

After a while Grastem began to believe, Myosin deliberately wanted to burn things.

Grastem could never forget the time she burned Rozel; Myosin would shoot flames up in the air. Rozel teased her, splashing water in the air putting out her flames. This would always result in a battle. With Rozel having the water ability, he assumed he had the advantage. Myosin's anger grew from Rozel's torment. She let a huge burst of flames out. Grastem never knew she even possessed this amount of power. The flames warped the garden and Rozel along with it. Rozel's scream echoed throughout the castle. Everyone rushed to the garden. Rozel was on his knees gripping his right arm which was covered in burned marks. Ithilia ran to Rozel, taking him and flying off. Baggasin then grabbed Myosin and forced her into the kingdom, pushing and shoving her. Myosin was begging for forgiveness, she kept restating that she didn't know that would happen. Myosin was quickly silenced when Father struck her across her face. That was the first time Baggasin hit any of them. Myosin was in shock. Salomne and Grastem looked over Baggasin's shoulder as Ithilia and Rozel flew back in. Rozel had been healed. Everyone assumed the Fairies had done it, but the timing was to quick. After confessing that Rozel had healing abilities they weren't confused as to why were gone for only for a short period of time and he was healed.

Ithilia was storming over to Myosin, as she was still on the ground still in shock from being hit. She demanded that he apologize to Rozel. But Rozel didn't want an apology. He knew he had did wrong as well and being burned was his consequence.

Ithilia silenced Rozel, and kept demanding that Myosin apologize. Suddenly, Myosin stood up, looked them all in their eyes and said, "I will not apologize for who I am!" and zipped past them with her speed, outside the castle.

Grastem had followed Myosin, who was sitting on a ledge over a balcony. Grastem told her that he had witnessed everything and told their parents what really happened. She went on to tell Grastem, "I feel like you are my guardian angel, you are always the one who sees the good in me. You've never judged me and you have always been there. One day I will repay you."

Ever since then, Myosin hasn't been the same. She turned aggressive and vulgar.

During Bernard's speech, Grastem looked to his left and glanced at Myosin. He noticed a smirk on her face. Her eyes showed flames flaring, burning with a passion for something,. Grastem knew she was up to something, and was unsure if he wanted to be involved. Grastem leaned in to whisper in her ear, "Myosin, what are you up to?"

"Whatever do you mean, brother?" she asked with sarcasm.

"Whatever you plan on doing, cut it out. This is serious," Grastem warned her.

Myosin didn't respond. She still had a grin, as her leg bounced back to face Bernard.

CHAPTER 4

SNAKE IN THE GRASS

MYOSIN HAD A plan in the making. They were all standing in front of Bernard, because earlier that day, Myosin made Ithilia aware of the dreams Rozel has been having.

Ithilia was devastated when she found out that they have been going on for years and she had just now got word about them. She began to confide in Myosin about the battle they must do. How scared she was to have to watch them fight each other. Ithilia has no choice, Baggasins made the decision and now she must follow his wishes. She told Myosin that she needed her to go into the sanctuary and retrieve the scroll of legends.

The scroll of legends is a magical scroll. If asked any question it shall give the answer. It knows everything.

Ithilia wanted to ask it where she could find the Shakawa; An ancestry book. This should tell her about the history of the phigons, and the dreams previous phigons have had. That will answer the question as to why Rozel is having these dreams.

Myosin did what she was told and began to walk out of the room, into the hallway. The castle has many doors, bathrooms, bedrooms, nurseries, kitchens and numerous of other things.

The sanctuary, Myosin's favorite room, holds every book, scroll, and spell there is to know. The scroll of legends is kept in a glass volt. Clear, so it can be seen but not touched. But Myosin must break the glass to retrieve it.

Myosin punched right through the volt. The glass rang in her ears as it shattered all over the floor. She reached for the scroll and retrieved it. Her hands tingled while she gripped the scroll.

The scroll has this feeling of extraordinary power. When she held it, electricity shot through her body. It gave her chills. Before she left, she asked it where she could find the Shakawa. When she opened the scroll, a deep majestic voice called out. It told her it was in a crystal box, hidden in the cave located deep in the east of the Atlantic temple.

Myosin knew that she should get Rozel's help, given that he is the Water Phigon and can stay underwater for a long period of time. Faster and more efficient than anyone else she knows.

Rozel can easily be persuaded, especially by Myosin, and she knew he would help if this could give him the answers he wants.

Myosin wanted this book for herself. She knew in order to have the heir to the throne, she must have more knowledge about these battle before anyone else does. Unfortunately, she can't swim and never desired to learn because she felt she was weak under water. Rozel enjoys swimming with them, he can't communicate with them, but he sure knows how to interact with them. Myosin tends to show how envious she is whenever Rozel goes swimming. Wherever he goes, whatever he does, Rozel knows how to interact with anyone and anything. Myosin on the other hand, comes off very aggressive and offensive. People are often intimidated by her, when she only means to be humorous and entertaining. Grastem can learn anything within a matter of seconds. Salomne can get anyone he wants, he has been with several girls and guys.

Myosin occasionally says that she can barely get a bird to sing to her in the morning.

She is very good looking. Her skin is tan, but you can tell she is mixed. Her hair is long. Black and at the end she has bright orange streaks. Her eyes are amber. Myosin, only being 18, she has a lot of knowledge about the Phoenixes and fire properties. But she is very naive with thinking fire is the destruction element. She yearns to learn the ability to make her fire blue. She knows that's what's going to cause her victory in the battle just like the Phoenix King Wetchador. She loves attention, so she tends to tend to show off her ability to get it. But that tends to lead into someone getting hurt or angry with her for destroying something, so she shuns herself.

This is why she wants to be Queen. Everyone will have no other choice but to give her the attention she wants. She will have anyone she wants.

★ ★ ★

Myosin decided not to tell Ithilia about finding the book yet. Myosin wanted to have the first glance through the book. This way he may have the upper hand in winning the throne zone. Soon after Bernard was finished with training, Myosin looked to see that Rozel was walking up the stone steps back into the castle. She ran after him and pulled Rozel to the side and began to talk to him.

"Hey, Roze. Are you ready for the battle?" Myosin said out of breath, but enthusiastic.

"Hey Mye, honestly, I don't know. I'm just distracted by the dreams I have been having," he said.

"Yeah, I overheard your conversation with Salomne last night. Hey! I know a way to get answers," Myosin said comforting.

"Wait, you do? Tell me!" Roze said eagerly.

Myosin knew it was the perfect time to get that book.

When Myosin told him more about the information of the book, Roze couldn't have been happier.

"Quit jumping around like a wild beast, you're acting pretty, hmm how should I say, piteous," said Myosin. Her hands were crossed and her stance was as if she was looking above Rozel.

"Do you mean pitiful?" Roze corrected.

"Same difference!" Mye said irritated

Rozel then went on to tell Myosin that he wanted to keep this between her and Salomne. Myosin agreed. Although she didn't want to add Salomne in any plans of hers, she knew that if she wanted to be queen, she needed to show compassion for his family and Rozel's lucid dreams.

★ ★ ★

The Atlantic Castle is huge. It has a very traditional concept. Sitting at the peak of Spascic. Pillars help support how the castle stands. It is made up of black stones and molding them together is red glowing magma lights. Lilac Solanum crawls up the castle and covers half it. Water surrounds the castle, about 12 feet deep. Gillies, creatures who live in the lakes, seas, and oceans, fill the water. Gillies tend to migrate, they don't stand in one place. They are as big as dolphins. They are definitely a decent size, enough to feed a whole family.

CHAPTER 5

THE SHAKAWA

ROZEL AND MYOSIN finally made their way east, towards Atlantic Nation.

Atlantic Nation is home to the dragons and mermaids, along with other sea creatures who roam the waters. The castle building sits on top of a body of water, but the real empire is underwater. The building is tall and sea foam green. It has water lilies surrounding the water above it. The underwater empire has a clear dome looking out into the ocean. It is able to see all life underwater. The mermaid and dragon civilians love to swim past and wave at the shifters as they work. The dome protects them from any intruders and unwanted guests.

Myosin and Rozel fly right above the location the scroll told Myosin. They landing on a nearby ledge that hovers over the rushing water; hitting against the rocks below. They shift back into their human forms and Rozel looks the water aggressively smacking into the wall below them. It looked safer when they flying.

He is starting to feel hesitant and reluctant.

"Okay, I'm not sure why this is the area they decided to leave the book, but here we are. Are you ready?" said Myosin.

"Yeah I guess," Rozel said hesitantly. "Hey, Mye why do you want this book? It just seems random that you want me to help you," Rozel asked.

"Well, dearest young one," Myosin said to get under Rozel's skin. "This book is an ancestry journal. Maybe we can find out if the guy in your dreams is an ancestor in any of the royal kingdoms. It may explain why he has been haunting your dreams,"

"I guess." He paused. "But what if he isn't in the book what if-"

"Rozel, you worry too much. Let's take one thing at a time." Myosin said cutting off Rozel.

"Okay," Rozel said apprehensively.

He turned into his Phigon form. He is faster and stronger than he is when he is in his human form. His body has wings of a Dragon; long webbed and wide. Spikes point at the bottom of each wing, so sharp it could cut someone just by staring at them for too long, metaphorically speaking. His scales are blue and white. His body is as slim as a phoenix; as his chest sticks out and is pumped up similar to a bird's posture, standing on his two feet. The tail is drifted into seven feathers. When flicked his tail produces water droplets, splashing anyone in the vicinity.

Rozel dives into the water, it is refreshing and cold. Like a fresh cup of water after eating mints. His body heat warms up causing him to quickly be immune to the water. The water is turquoise and clear like the island shores rushing upon the beach. It shines bright, reflecting the sunlight. It's a tropical setting he is swimming through. The tides are strong, he can feel himself being pushed in the direction of the water, but the cave is in the opposite direction.

Rozel then spots a group of gillies swimming towards him, swiftly floating in the water. Rozel adores gillies. They are beautiful, and they are said to be related to the earth's dolphins. They are just as smart and charismatic.

One begins to swim up next to Rozel, and is swimming around him. His body is light grey and its fin sits high. It's a male. Females are more of a darker shade.

Rozel starts to notice that the gillie is gesturing for Rozel to follow him. He helps Rozel swim through the water, avoiding the tide the best way they can.

He is leading Rozel into the direction of a cave.

When they arrive, the cave's whole is too small for Rozel to go through, he won't be able to fit in, but the gillie can.

Something is glowing from inside, he signals Rozel to stay where he is, circling around him to stop. He swims inside the cave to obtain the glowing object.

After a while, Rozel began to notice that the gillie was taking quite some time, and Myosin isn't a very patient gal. But just before Rozel began to lose hope, the Gillie comes out. Something is in his mouth as it shimmers in the light. He comes closer and Rozel sees a book inside a crystal box. The Shakawa. The gillie places it in Rozel's giant tongue. It's so salty from the ocean. The Gillie nods his head, out of joy. Rozel does the same as a 'thank you' for his service. Rozel swims to the surface, wondering how the gillie knew he was looking for the book.

Within seconds, he makes his way through the waters of the ocean back to the surface where he sees Myosin sitting down on the beaches shore letting the waves hit her feet.

Rozel flies out of the water, and makes his way towards Myosin, with the box in his mouth tasting like a brick of salt on his tongue.

When he makes it to Myosin, he spits it out at Myosin forcing her to fall backwards when she catches it. Rozel's wings cover his mouth as he lets out an amplified laugh. He shifts back to his human form, he couldn't help but laugh when he noticed Myosin struggling to get back up.

Suddenly, Rozel sees steam coming out from the box in her hand. She was melting the crystal box that surrounded the book.

"Be careful, Mye, don't burn the book," Rozel said cautiously.

"Relax, I know what I'm doing," Myosin muttered.

Rozel saw the box was incinerated. The book was released.

He runs over to Myosin and looks at her face as it lit up. Rozel never saw Myosin this happy before. This is a first time in such a long time that they were able to share a smile.

"What now?" Rozel said.

"Now we read." Myosin started to flip the pages. They are crinkled and brown. It had been down there for over a century. "There has to be something about that guy."

They flip through about ten pages and still had found nothing. They wondered if anything will be found.

"Maybe if we ask it a question it will give us an answer," Rozel said, he was leaning over. He was interrupted when Myosin snatched the book away.

"This isn't the legend of scrolls Rozel, this is a book. We have to find the answers on our own," he said aggressively. He placed it back in front of them. "Is there anything you can tell me, any details about this guy? Anything specific?" he said still flipping through pages, his eyes still planted on the book.

"He is tall, um his hair was curly and had brown skin. I never got a glimpse of his face because I seem to keep my distance in the dream. But I do remember when he took steps; he left ice shards sparkling on the ground."

"Ice shards? Okay. Hold on, maybe we can find something about ice shards." Determined, she flipped the pages faster. Rozel watched as she went page by page.

"Wait. Stop!" Rozel said abruptly. "I saw something, I think."

Myosin started to turn the pages back. "It was right…. Here!" Rozel shouted.

He pointed to a page that had a snowflake on the top right corner of the book. It didn't take much of the page but underneath it had a crown. "He must've been royalty, Mye!"

"But that doesn't explain the snowflake," Myosin continued reading, skimming through the words with her finger while her eyes followed. "Here," she pointed, "it says he was like no other. Neither Dragon nor Phoenix but had the characteristics of both," she said eagerly. He looked over at Rozel "Sound familiar?" She continued, "Their beast form stood on up like the flaming bird, but had the scaly wings of the mighty dragon. His wings were white and fluttered snowflakes when flapped. Its body was covered in white scales and its tail stretched ending with two clear balls of ice. Xui and his twin brother Zender were the last two Phigons to be born before the subjeckies slaughtered every single one that was alive." Myosin looked over towards Rozel concerned. "Well at least we know names, their names…" She read on. "When he was born he was like a block of ice; cold. Soon he began to develop powers of snow. He was able to conjure up ice from his hands forming it into any object he desired. His skin was cold; he walked around with a trail of fog, as if he was being melted. He had a tending to leave ICY SHARDS when he took steps!" She looked at Rozel with excitement in her voice. "Rozel, we found our answer!"

"Yes!" Rozel shouted. "But who is he? Why is he altering my dreams?"

"We are getting there. Come on, there is more to read." She nudged him and kept reading. "Their father was the Great Phoenix King Wetchador and their mother was Flocean, one of the most powerful Dragons to ever live. So powerful she was named Mother of Dragons. When he saw that his sons were a threat to his power; Wetchador decided that no Phigon should be born again and killed any remaining Phigons alive including his son Zender.

Xui was trying to access his powers but his anxiety was blinding his concentration. He was afraid that he lost control of his powers while hiding undergrounds. Meanwhile outside, he caused a massive blizzard that swept the nation. The plains were covered in snow. Hail shot from the sky, cutting the civilians. It felt like glass falling from the sky, piercing anyone who was outside. Many people kept inside, because the snow was so cold. It was acidic touching it, burning the people to their deaths."

"Wait, did it- I felt that in my dream. In a cave, it was covered in ice all around. When I touched it, I heard sizzling and I gripped my hand. When I looked, I saw steam evaporate from my hand as my flesh melted off. Luckily my ability healed myself. But I felt the pain, I felt like I was there, Mye."

Rozel looked at her, disturbed at what he was reading. This was the guy he has been seeing. "Skim through and see what happened to him."

"It says his brother Zender caused a storm of lighting to appear right before his death. It was called the dark storm. Zender…" She paused; her eyes were squinted, observing the page more.

"What? Zender, what?" said Rozel.

"Zender possessed the power of lightning. He struck Wetchador with a bolt leaving a scar on his chest." She looked at Rozel. "So, the scar on Wetchador's chest wasn't a birthmark, why would the hide this from the world?"" He was speaking softly. His words drifted into a mumble.

"Myosin, what is going on?" Rozel called out

"They're like us." She looked concerned. "Unique beasts? Substantial abilities? Ice powers, Lightning and storms? Roze, these are traits that we possess"

"Yeah, but why haven't we heard of them? If they had this much significance, why aren't they mentioned?" Rozel asked.

"You're asking the wrong person, maybe they kept it from the world to protect us," she answered.

"Well I was referring you to find out." Rozel rolled his eyes, as he pointed to the book.

"It doesn't say, moron, or I would've told you," she said aggressively. "Maybe they wanted to erase this part of history. It sounds like this was something catastrophic, maybe they wanted to cover it up," she replied.

"Does it say what happened to them?"

"Not much," she said and squinted and eased closer down to the book. "It says after his brother was killed the leader of the Fairies, Myrtle Merlow went to find the last phigon, and help him escape Wetchador's rage. She vanished, never heard or seen again. But it was found that she had ancient spells, to work on creating a new world from a star. Similar to how Spascic was created." she said.

"I know this may be a little far-fetched but what if he was taken to a star, as in The Burning Star?!" Rozel asked.

"Wow, this is crazy, and Wetchador killed his own son because of power." He looked up and went into thought. "I may find you guys annoying but I couldn't kill any of my family, at least I don't think I would?"

"I'm just going to assume that was an endearing statement because you love your family." Rozel just looked at him for a moment, his face show my emotion of annoyance for him.

"Well it came from the heart...anyways, it says Zender's body was never found and there was no trace of Xui found underground either." He turned the page back and forth as if he was looking for something. "There is nothing about Zender. Xui has a whole segment about him, but nothing about Zender." Myosin was distracted, flipping through pages.

Rozel looked off into the distance. He could hear the swishing of the crinkling pages. "I'm going to go look for him on the burning star." He said randomly as slap his shorts, dusting the sand off his shorts.

"Wait, what?! Rozel, you don't even know if this stuff is true. What do you think Mother would say if you just up and left? She would have a heart burst, and Dad. Ha, you would be even lucky to step your toes outside again."

"I wasn't asking for permission," he demanded; he had gotten this far and he wanted all his questions answered. Rozel was determined to get them.

Myosin slammed the book closed and started getting up. She stood over Rozel, shading him from the sun and didn't have a pleasing look on her face. "Hey, I'm all for you getting your 'answers' or whatever, but I don't want you ending up somewhere you aren't supposed to be and I get blamed, as usual."

"Come on, Mye," he begged. "I needed these answers, and I feel haunted by these dreams and want them to stop."

She looked off into the distance for a moment.. "Alright, I will cover for you, but not today. This weekend-" When she looked back she looked defeated.

"The weekend?!" he interrupted.

"Yes this weekend. Look, I will help you but I'm not going to be the last person seen with you if something does happen. I will not be blamed. You want these answers, go get them, I will cover for you and say that you are going to meet everyone at the festival. You have one hour and then come back."

"One hour, at least give me three hours."

"Two and that's it."

"Fine."

"Leave at noon, that way it won't seem suspicious. Everyone will be distracted by the festivities they won't notice you're not there."

Rozel hugged and thanked her. He had never seen this side of her before. However, Rozel couldn't help but to think that Myosin had an ulterior motive.

Later that day, they returned home. Myosin avoided Ithilia, so she did not have to give up the book until she had enough information.

Throughout the week, Salomne notices that Myosin and Rozel have been getting closer each day that. He begins to get a little worried about them hanging out with each other. It is not typical to find them hanging with each other without fighting. In the past, Salomne once told Grastem that he feels Myosin has a vendetta against Rozel after the incident of getting burned. Salomne has tried to get close to Rozel, ever since they found out about the next Andromeda. Their elemental powers are stronger than Myosin and Grastem.

When Rozel started to have lucid dreams, Salomne made it an priority to be there for him. Rozel has has become more annoyed than grateful, he could never full see out his dreams because Salomne is there shaking him awake.

Truth be told, Salomne doesn't trust Myosin, and now that Myosin has been getting close to Rozel, he also envy's their relationship. It has progressed more in a few days than Salomne's relationship has in years.

CHAPTER 6

THE VISION

THE DOORBELL RINGS, it echoes in the halls like a siren. Salomne is in his room reading his scrolls.

Grastem went to help set up for the festival. It was the next night. He does every festival.

No one was near the door to answer it quickly. The bell rings again and Salomne yells, "Coming!" He is making his way down the hall, to the door.

The castle in the Volcanic Tribe is made up of two floors. Its interior has 15 rooms, all used for different things, and 12 wash rooms. It also has a Spiritual Garden, where sun flowers grow. Phoenixes believe sun flowers are a sacred gift from the Gods; they absorb energy from the sun, just like the phoenixes.

When Salomne makes his way through the hall and down the stairs, he notices Baggasin standing at the top of the stairs talking with Celia, daughter of the Queen of Fairold, Violet. Celia is said to be as powerful as the great Myrtle Merlow.

Her hair looks black from a distance but is really dark purple. Very long, and straight falling down her back. She tucks the left side of her hair behind her ear. Sparkles from the fairy's sand glisten in her hair as it reflects off the sun light that creeps in the house. She is not that tall, her head touches Salomne's chest. She has beautiful caramel skin. About 20 years old, and can heal anything she touches, similar to Rozel's ability. She also has the gift of seeing visions of the future, and she has never been wrong.

Salomne takes a great liking to her.

He starts to gallop down the stairs at the sight, ecstatic to see her. He notices she was bothered with something. Her face showed her fear. Salomne knew she had a vision.

Celia had seen something terrible.

Persistent, Salomne runs down the stairs to see what was wrong, Celia and Baggasin notices him skipping down a lot of step. He isn't aware that his feet didn't plant on the steps correctly. He loses his balance and falls down the stairs. He spirals down like kids on a hill. As he tumbles down, he grunts on each stair case.

When he stops at the bottom, his head is at her feet. Looking down at him, Baggasin bursts out in laughter. Celia giggles as she helps Salomne up, making sure he is okay. Salomne is dusting off whatever dirt he had collected on his way down the stairs.

"Hey," he said grabbing his right arm, "what are you doing here?"

"She had a vision Salomne. She wanted to come warn us about it," Baggasin answered.

"What kind of vision?" He looked towards Celia.

"He isn't a man, he looked about 20 years old or so," Celia described. "He may appear to be a young, but he holds remarkable power. Similar to you and your brothers," she said, referring to Salomne.

"Celia said that she felt him in her vision, and he was very cold," chimed in Baggasin.

Salomne begins to worry, "Do you know why you might be having this vision?"

"He's coming. Here… I can't explain it but I sensed his aura. He gave off a disturbed vibe."

"Why is he coming, Celia? What is he after?" said Baggasin.

"That's just it. I don't know. But I feel he may be a threat to Spascic." Her voice changed weary. Tears fell down her face, and her voice started to crack. "I—I saw myself." She stopped and looked down.

"What did you see, Celia!?" Baggasins demanded.

"Father," Salomne silenced Baggasins, "what did you see?" he said comforting Celia. He grabbed her and held her.

She was shaking. Salomne could sense her fear.

Celia lifted her hands onto his face and closed her eyes. Suddenly, Salomne's eyes started to glow. He felt her vision projecting in his mind.

He started to see into Celia's head:

> *There was the guy she was talking about. He was standing in the doorway of the Sanctuary of Prayers. Celia's body was being consumed*

inside a crystal of ice. Growing every minute, trapping her. Her neck had bruises as if she was previously choked. Her back had scratches and cuts.

Celia's blood had been dripping from her back down onto the ice. The guy was watching her as the ice grew more and more. You couldn't see his face entirely, the sun was shadowing his face, but Salomne did see that he had a smile on his face. Celia was trying to reach for her elixirs to remove the ice, but it just grew faster the more she moved.

She stopped struggling to free herself. She was growing faint. The ice had reached her waist, capturing her hands. The young man turned away, walking out the door.

Celia had pulled her hands away. "Now you know." She said. Her voice turned strong. She stood tall wiping away her tears. "I will not allow this to happen. By any means."

In fear of what he saw, Salomne held onto her passionately.

Distraught, he couldn't stomach what he had seen. He let go of her and grabbed onto her elbows and looked her into her eyes. "I promise, I will not let anything happen to you." He pulled her into his arms and hugged her once more. He didn't want to believe in her vision, but he knew none of her visions had been false. Salomne was in over his head making a promise like that, and was not confident that he would be able to keep it.

"We will look into this, Celia, don't you worry." Baggasins patted her back and walked past them. Turning back, he looked at Salomne. "Salomne, gather your brothers, make them aware of these visions. We need to be careful from now on."

Salomne nodded his head. Celia thanked him. She got on her tippy toes and planted a kiss onto him.

It was a magical moment for him.

Celia stepped away from him and threw pebbles onto the ground, causing a cloud of smoke to appear; warping her into it. When the smoke cleared up, Celia was gone. She had teleported back to Fairold.

CHAPTER 7

FESTIVITIES

T HE NEXT DAY was the day of the Festival. The festival celebrates the peace in the world, the coming together of all kingdoms, moving on from the reign and destruction of Wetchador.

Taking back the independence of their nation and putting a stop to the fear he left them with.

For events, the residents in the castle usual go out into the city of Jubar, which is right outside the castle. Fairies arrive and they sprinkle fairy sand on the ground to help make the plants grow. They start to glow a mystical, beautiful turquoise, purple, and silver light.

The Airians fly down from the air pyramids. They use bow and arrows to shoot fireworks in the sky announcing that the festival has started.

When the night comes, the phoenixes fly in the sky. They open their flaming wings, lighting up the sky like the sun. From their mouths, they spit fire into a giant pit; Staring a bonfire that brightens up the whole city. The fire has beautiful colors of yellow, amber, orange, and red. The fire cracks making a snapping sound. The ember dances off the fire, dimming into the dirt.

★ ★ ★

Drina, Grastem's best friend, is from the western air pyramid. She has an Egyptian look to her. Her skin is creamed coffee. Her eyes are green and outlined with black eyeliner. Gold dots the tip where her eyeliner ends. She is in charge of all of the festivities.

Drina wrote a letter to Grastem to see if he would like to help set up.

The letter was sent it using girties, hawk like creatures. Letters are attached to them so they can deliver and pass on messages. That was the Airians way of sending messages.

Drina knows Grastem isn't going to say no. Grastem loves setting up festivals. He is also a big help when he uses his earth ability to create vines and flowers that make banners that are hung to decorate the buildings.

Hans, a young man about 19 years old, also helps set up. He is dragon, from the Atlantic Nation.

Grastem takes a liking to him. He is taller than Grastem. He is, about 6'2. His skin is always tanned from him being out in the sun a lot. His hair is shaved on the sides but is curly black on the top. The colors of his eyes are light brown and he has tattoos on both arms; Grastem never really pays any attention to them because he's more focused on his muscular body.

Hans' voice is deep but soft. His smile is bright and captivating, and his lips are full and red; he does a weird movement to them when he thinks. He bites the inside of his cheek and moves his lips up and down.

Hans met Grastem during past events. They have previously worked together on the decorations. Hans knows how to sew really well, so Grastem conjures plants from the ground so he could sew them into a banner to hang around the city.

When Wetchador was ruling, liking the same sex was banned. You would be executed for being a 'freak' that was gay. The new ruler Kueir, King of the Air Pyramids, has no problem with sexuality. He, himself is bisexual, and he tends lay down with anyone he sets his eyes onto. Being that he is king, it doesn't take a lot for him to seduce anyone. Most civilians throw themselves at him.

But Kueir feels that he should not be seen for whom he lies down with but for how he rules.

This has caused a lot of peace throughout Spascic. Kueir has been in power for over 9 decades, but to the people of Spascic it only feels like 9 years. He won the Andromeda with his Pegasus, Vira, and his mighty bow and arrow that are now framed in his bedroom.

Hans' sexuality is unidentified. He has been only seen with girls, but a lot of guys flirt with him. Grastem has been trying to go out with him many times but because many girls and guys are all over Hans, Grastem doesn't have the opportunity to ask.

Grastem notices Hans doesn't act the same way to other people like he does towards him.

When Grastem arrives to the setting, Drina is telling everyone that she is putting them into groups of two. She has a sheet of names on them, and she was calling out for people to join their partner.

Grastem's name comes up…

"Grastem?" Drina said looking for him in the crowd.

Grastem looks up and smirks. This was the chance to be paired with Hans. He gave off a little wink to declare his rightful position as Hans' partner.

She goes on, "Grastem you will be paired with….. Nittia."

His own best friend partnered him with Nittia, a phoenix girl who is obsessively in love with Rozel. Grastem's jaw dropped. He felt betrayed. His hopes were hooked on being partnered with Hans.

He questioned their friendship at this point.

Drina continued calling out the names. "Hans, you will be paired off with Flana."

Grastem's annoyance for Drina grew. He looked to the left where Flana was standing. As she jumps up and down like a schoolgirl joining the cheerleading team.

He looks back at Drina; she is standing up on the podium giggling.

Soon after everyone is paired off, Grastem rushed over to where Drina was standing.

"What was that?!" he whispered aggressively.

"Remember that time you forgot to take me with you to Havik to see my crush Kosie? Well this is payback." She said jabbing him with her finger.

"Yeah, okay, I get it." He throws his hands up in defeat. "But did you have to pair me with Nittia?! You didn't think taking Hans wasn't enough?!" Drina was still laughing as she noticed Grastem's frustration. "Oh you find this funny?" he said. "I wonder if you would find me slapping you with some lilies funny," he added, aggressively.

"Actually, she paid me to pair you with her. I wanted to give you Crust over there." Crust is a giant smelly Ogre. His stench travels for miles. They both turn their heads to look over at Crust, he has slobber coming off his mouth and snorts up a huge snot bubble back into his nose right before he wipes his mouth off with his sleeve. "Maybe it's the Gods saving you," she said, comforting.

"They are going to save you." He started to grow lilies from the ground. The stems grow tall enough for him to pluck them out of the ground. Swinging his arm back he was getting ready to hit her with the lilies. But just before he could attack her, Nittia ran up behind him.

"Hey, Grastem, whatcha doing?" she said. Grastem fixed his mouth to reply but she cut him off, "Oh nothing, cool. I'm soooo happy to be working with you today. Are you happy to be working with me...? Oh of course you are." She talks so quickly cutting off every questions with her own answers.

Grastem looks over to Drina, she smirks, waving as she begins to scurry off. "We should get started, we have A LOT to do," said Nittia.

She grabs Grastem, and forces him into a chair not too far from where they were standing. Their view of Hans was clear, he was working with Flana straight across. Hans was doing all the work sewing the vines he collected together.

Flana is a very popular girl because of her looks. She is gorgeous. She has short black hair, with bangs. Her eyes are blue. Her body is curvy, her hips are wide and her butt is firm. She has the whole package.

Grastem can't help but look over at him. His eyes are being pulled to look at him, like magnets.

Nittia jumps in front of his view of Hans, "So, how is Rozel? Is he good? Does he think about me?" she said, interrupting his daydream.

"Have you ever thought about asking, oh I don't know, one question at a time?" Grastem quickly replied. "Plus, I have no idea if Rozel thinks about you. You are talking to Grastem and not Rozel as you can see, go ask him yourself." Grastem was moving his head to look past Nittia. Hans spotted him looking. He grinned at Grastem and just before Grastem could catch his breath, Hans winked at him. Grastem attempted to wink back at him, but his glasses began sliding off. He felt like a fool when Hans laughed. Grastem turned away in embarrassment.

"Who's that?!" said Nittia

"Huh? Who him? No one," Grastem said nervously, and turned away.

She tapped Grastem and said, "I was talking about her but glad to know it's the guy." He was busted.

"I don't want to talk about it," he replied.

Nittia shrugged her shoulders and continued plucking the flowers.

Soon after the setting up was done, Grastem went to find Drina. She was talking to Kosie and she looked happy.

He didn't want to disturb her, just in case something else like this happens. He went off walking back towards the gate entrance, back to his home. When he made it to the gates, he heard his name being called from the distance. Grastem turned around and it was Hans running after him.

"Hey, where you going?" he asked.

"Back home, the festival is starting soon and I need to start getting ready," Grastem replied.

"So, that answers my next question, I will see you tonight," he said.

"Well, that depends on if you want to or not," he said confidently. He poked his nose up and laid his hands on his hips. His glasses started to slide down again so he broke his posture to adjust.

"Oh shut up, you know I do." He gently punched his shoulder.

Grastem smiled and chuckled as he grabbed his shoulder. "Well I guess I will see you tonight then," he said backing away.

"Hey wait," Hans said quickly. "Do you want to go together? Maybe." His voice sounded anxious.

"Um." Grastem's body got warm and he started to blush. He was caught off guard. "Yes!" he shrieked. Hans chuckled as he looked down, noticing that Grastem's hand was covering himself. He was aroused from the excitement.

Hans smiled as he wiped his nose off with his thumb with confidence.

"Okay, I'll meet you at your castle then and we can fly out here together." He turned away and winked.

"Yeah, sure." Grastem was embarrassed. His body was still but he felt like he melted into a puddle of water.

On the walk home, Grastem couldn't stop smiling, though he was embarrassed he was too excited from Hans asking him out to let anything defeat him.

Grastem looked further out in the distance. He had a long way from the castle and walking wouldn't give him enough time to get ready. Flying there was his best bet, so he changed into a Phigon.

Grastem's phigon form has dark majestic green scales that cover his body. His tail ends with the flower Anthurium. When he flaps his wings, petals falls off gliding in the wind.

He has the most artistic look.

Myosin has amber scales. Her tail ends with a flame. When she flaps her wings, she give off ember.

Salome has more of royal look. His scales are silver and gold. His tail ends with a puffy white cloud. When he flaps his wings, a gust of wind sparkles gold glitter that falls on his back.

When Grastem makes it back to the castle, he immediately runs to his room to sort through his outfits.

CHAPTER 8

THE BAD NEWS

SALOMNE IS SITTING in the living room. There is a second floor visible showing the balcony used to fly in and out of the castle. He notices that Rozel and Myosin are talking, making their way down the stairs. Grastem starts to fly in on the balcony.

Rozel turns his head and sees Salomne waiting for them. Excited to share the news with him, Rozel runs down the stairs making his way over to Salomne. "Hey, Salomne! I have something to tell you."

"As do I." Salomne could see Grastem gliding down towards his landing. "I want to wait until Grastem lands. He needs to hear this too."

"What's wrong? You seem upset about something," said Myosin.

"I am. I'm very distraught," he said.

"Wait, what does that mean?" asked Myosin.

"It means that his mind wanders because he's preoccupied," said Rozel. Both Salomne and Myosin looked over at him. He seemed so confident and cheerful when he said it. "That means we have to be more interesting like how Celia is." Rozel was the only one who laughed.

"No it doesn't, that's distracted, you moron." Myosin said.

"Hey," Salomne said looking at Myosin, defending Rozel. "Distraught means I'm upset." He looked over at Grastem. "Here comes Grastem." He flew down and shifted. His face was glowing. "I'm glad one of us is in a good mood."

"I'm in a good mood, a fantastic mood if I might add," Myosin said taking the shine. She turned to Rozel, "Rozel, are you in a good mood?" she asked sarcastically.

"GREAT!" Rozel shouted throwing his hands in the air.

"Best friends I see." Salomne said under his breath. His jealousy was obvious. Grastem was walking towards them. Salomne looked over at Grastem. "I'm glad you are all here. I need to tell you about Celia's vision."

"She had a vision? It's been quite a while since we heard that she had a vision. What was it about?" Grastem asked.

"She was trapped. I think she was dying." His heart sank down his body when he said it aloud. He felt like he had already lost her.

"Wait, hold on. She was dying?! How?" Myosin interrupted, she seemed excited.

"She was stuck in ice made from the guy described by the dream you've been having Rozel."

"Speaking of my dreams-" Rozel included. Myosin quickly nudged him to stop him from revealing what they had found out.

She gave a look to Rozel and turned back to listen to Salomne. "Continue, brother…"

Salomne ignored her nudging him went on, "He was standing in the doorway of the sanctuary, and was smiling at the ice growing more and more, trapping her body. Blood raced down her back, and her neck looked as if she had been chocked." His voiced cracked

"Wait, whose blood was it?" said Rozel.

"Celia's, Rozel. Who else would be bleeding? You?" said Myosin.

"Listen" said Salomne, "This guy is coming and we need to protect Celia. Because we are the strongest creatures on this planet, the four of us can protect her."

"Yeah, but Salom-" Rozel attempted to say something, but Myosin interrupted. "Ow, Mye. What was that for?" She stomped on his left foot to shut him up.

Myosin grinned at Salomne and asked, "What do you need us to do?"

"Um," Salomne was confused. "Just be around for the right moment. We need to be on guard. I can't lose Celia." He was wondering why she was cutting Rozel off so much

"Can't lose something you never had," Myosin said, laughing.

"Oh come on, Myosin," Grastem chimed in. "Don't be an ass right now."

Myosin shrugged and walked away. It didn't bother Salomne. He was more bothered by Rozel chasing after her, assuming their conversation was over.

"When did they become so close?" Salomne asked himself.

Grastem attempted to reply, but Salomne walked away leaving Grastem alone, and speechless.

CHAPTER 9

A BROTHER S LOYALTY

A FEW MOMENTS LATER, Ithilia calls for Rozel to come into her makeup room. There were guards in her entrance.

"Pardon me, sir," Rozel said to one of them.

"Yes my lord," replied the guard as he stepped aside.

When he made it into the room he saw Salomne sitting with his head down. Ithilia stood, walking towards Rozel.

"Rozel, sit." She pulled him into the room further, directing his movements into a chair that was at the end of her dresser. "I sent for you. Your siblings have made me aware of the dreams you have been having. A boy in an ice kingdom." She sounded so concerned and confused.

Salomne's eyes glanced over at Rozel, he knew he broke his promise.

Rozel grew angry, "Salomne?!" he whispered aggressively. He clenched his hands into a ball.

"Why have you kept this a secret from me? Did I wrong you of your trust?" Ithilia said expressing her disappointment.

"I didn't think anything of it, Mother." Rozel turned his face towards the door. He was embarrassed.

"So, why did you acknowledge this to your brother not your father and I?" she said persistently.

"Mother…" Rozel paused in search for words. He didn't want to blow his cover before he even gets the chance to go on his quest. He wanted her mind off of this subject, so he had to lie about his dream. "I entrusted him with a folktale. Every night he is there watching as I sleep. These dreams don't mean anything. I was testing his loyalty, and clearly he has failed." His eyes were still planted at the door.

"A folktale that has drifted from your nightmares into Celia's visions." She said getting frustrated.

Rozel turns towards Salomne. "You break your promise because of Celia's visions? A girl whom you have no clue loves you or not. You have no idea if this 'vision' is true. You would sacrifice your loyalty with me so you could help her!" His voice was growing louder. "You speak of loving one another. You always say, 'We must stick together' but you don't even practice what you preach."

"Salomne!" Mother said shocked.

"He brought this upon yourself. He would throw me away, so he can live in this magical fantasy, with someone who likes him one day and ignores him another."

"I was protecting you. Plus mother already knew because of your best friend Myosin."

"Are you really that jealous?" Rozel asked rhetorically. "This is Celia's threats, Salomne." Rozel was so infuriated. Celia's visions have never been wrong, but his anger running blocked him from caring if it was true or not.

This made him all the more curious to find out if Xui was real.

"Rozel, he was doing what was best for the family," Ithilia pleaded.

"No, Mother, he was doing what was best for him. This is what he does." Rozel looked away from Ithilia and looked into Salomne's eyes. "You have made a big mistake."

Rozel stood up. Ithilia grabbed his arm stopping him from leaving. He yanked away from Ithilia's grasp, storming past the guards and left the room.

Rozel went into his room and gathered supplies for his quest. He didn't have any more patience to wait until the festival. He needed to go that instant.

Within a matter of minutes, Rozel had everything he needed. It was his first time traveling outside of Spascic. His older siblings have, but he was too young. He decided it was his time.

He looked out his window, and below was a lake that surrounded the castle. Rozel jumped right into it. Under the water he transformed into his Phigon. His scales are aquamarine and they glimmered when they reflect the suns light. His tail ends like a mermaid, making it easier for him to swim in the water. When his wings burst out, water droplets rain down.

Rozel swims around back of the castle where Myosin's room is, thinking the coast would be clear. He shoots out the lake with jet speed and takes off.

CHAPTER 10

DEPARTURE

MYOSIN LOOKS OUT his window at Rozel as he sets off.

She is reading the Shakawa. It holds many stories of the past. How the creatures of the world migrated from earth. Now on earth they are considered, mythical creature. How the nations have evolved into what they are today. It tells talks about Solajark and Lalunas, ancient Gods.

It also talks about how the Andromeda came to be.

It shows previous kings and queens of Spascic. Dracos of the Dragons, was a mighty King of Spascic, Gertrude of Fairold who became queen soon after. Henry of the Air Pyramids, Tremar of Fairold, Robert of Volcanic Tribe and many years later Wetchador soon became King. Ithilia, mother of Phoenix, became the first female in the Volcanic Tribe to rule Spascic. All were victorious in the battle of the Andromeda.

The festival is a few hours away. Myosin's eyes are glued to the book and her time to get ready is running out. The more she reads the more engaged she is. Each victor has had a strategy, a technique, a plan.

A thought runs through her head; because each one of her brothers will be a representative for each nation's kingdom, will she have to hold back?

She looks up off into the distance. The sun was setting and the clouds were fuchsia.

Myosin notices something flying at her window, it was Rozel turning around. He headed toward her room.

Her head rises towards the ceiling and his eyes roll from his annoyance. Rozel had shifted and landed into her room. "Oh please come in, I wasn't busy or anything." She said.

"I've come to tell you that I know you went to mother about my dreams." Myosin was afraid that she had lost Rozel's trust too. "But I forgive you. You were not the one who made a promise to me." Myosin exhaled out of relief when she heard him say that. "I also came to let you know that I am headed out now."

"Wait what?!" Myosin positioned herself towards him. "Rozel, this was not the plan."

"I understand, Mye. But I-"

"But nothing, Roze. I agreed to covering for you, but how will I be able to cover for you if everyone is supposed to arrive at the festival together."

"Just say I am with Jezzy and we are arriving together. No one will notice I'm not there."

"This festival is for the nations coming together. Plus we are getting acknowledge as the new leaders in the Andromeda. And if it hasn't clicked in your mind yet, you're going to represent the Atlantic Nation. They will notice you missing."

"I will only be gone for the amount of time you've given me." Rozel pleaded.

"Roze, I don't think this is a good idea."

"Mye, if I don't go now, I won't be able to go at all. Mother will have her eyes me all the time, now that she knows about my dreams. Thank you by the way."

"Fiiinnneeee. But you only have two hours. Make it back to the festival before they announce our names."

"You have my word." He started to sprint out the room, he stopped and looked over his shoulder. "I don't know why Salomne has never trusted you." Rozel turned around and looked into Myosin's eyes, "You have been more loyal to me within the past day than he has been throughout my lifetime. I greatly appreciate you, Mye."

"As do I, brother." She shooed him away.

He jump out the window. Myosin ran after him, she was afraid he wouldn't be able to turn fast enough. But Myosin could hear his transformation happening. The sound of his wings flapped, and the water droplets slapped her in the face. She wiped her face and look to see him set off once more.

Rozel's words kept running through Myosin's mind. She couldn't understand why Salomne had his personal vendetta towards her either.

Even now, they are cordial but not close. She feared that they would never be.

CHAPTER 11

DATE NIGHT

I T'S ALMOST SUNDOWN, and the Festival is
about to start. The royal families, of each Kingdom
wait until everyone has arrived, so they can make their
grand entrance. It is a tradition.

With Rozel storming off, Ithilia and Baggasin figured
he wouldn't want to join them. So they weren't surprised
when Myosin informed them that he was going to be
with Jizzy.

Also Grastem is going out with Hans, which means
the tradition would be broken.

Hans is arriving shortly and Grastem is currently
getting ready. He is wearing his best suit. It's dark green
and shines when light hits it. The fabric is velvet. It grips

his waist and flows out when it ends. It will definitely catch Hans' eyes.

The doorbell rings through the halls. Grastem failed to mention to his father that he would be going with him. So when Baggasin opened the door to find that Hans had been waiting outside. He was confused.

"Your Majesty," Hans greeted as he bowed.

"Hans, what are you doing here? Shouldn't you be at the festival?" Baggasin said.

"I am here to pick up Grastem." He was wearing a blue sleeveless vest. It was loose around the arms but gripped his chest, showing off his muscles.

"Pick up Grastem? He is arriving with the family."

"Sin, let him go," Ithilia said kissing Baggasins on the cheek. She held onto his arm and faced Hans, "Hello, Hans."

"Your Highness." He bowed.

"Grastem should be ready by now. I'll go grab him." She said.

Ithilia turned to go grab Grastem, who was already making his way down the stairs.

When he came into the grand hall, the look his father gave him had devastation written all over it. He couldn't look him in the eyes, he knew that he had broken his heart.

Grastem greeted Hans with a bow. Hans grabbed his hands and lifted it as he bowed. Baggasin hugged Grastem. "I will see you there, Father." Grastem giggled and hugged Baggasin back. Baggasins wanted him to have a good time, even though he wasn't going to be with the family. Then he turned to Ithilia to do the same. "Love you guys both... now bye."

He shut the door behind him and turned to Hans. "Sorry about that, I forgot to tell them about us going together." His tone was high and flirtatious.

"It's my honor; I had to take the most powerful person in the land, and the cutest." Hans was trying to keep his wall up, but in the inside he was nervous.

"I wouldn't say that," Grastem said.

Hans looked at him with his endearing eyes. "Don't sell yourself short, you're really cute."

Grastem laughed. "No," he laughed. "I wouldn't say I'm the most powerful person. But cutest…cutest I will agree." They both shared a laugh as they continued to walk. "Did you want to fly there? I feel like it will be a while before we get there on foot." Grastem added.

"I don't mind walking, we can get to know each other more. If that's okay with you." He replied with a smile.

Grastem was so taken by his lips that he didn't pay attention to where he was stepping. There was a crack in the ground that indented. Without knowing, he stepped on it and tripped.

Hans grabbed his arm pulling him back up, catching him before he fell. "Maybe flying would be the best thing." Laughing, Hans shifted into a dragon. Grastem followed him when he turned into a phigon.

The festival had started. Fireworks were bursting in the sky and the bonfire was lit up.

Grastem flew down. When he shifted, he looked around and saw Drina talking to Korie. He ran up to her.

"Hey Drina." He said.

"Hey, Grastem, you made it." She looked over Grastem's left shoulder and saw Hans walking up to him. "You made it with Hans." She nudged him and smiled. "Why didn't you tell me!"

"You were too busy with kissing Korie's ass," he said, laughing. Drina didn't find it funny, as she punched him in the arm. "Ow! watch the suit, it's new"

"Sorry, Your Highness." Hans caught up to them and stood next to Grastem. "Hey Hans, fancy seeing you here." Drina said.

"I had to come with his greatness," Hans replied as he bowed.

"Stop that." Grastem pushed him up from his bow. He pushed his glasses up and looked around for any more familiar faces. Salomne was talking to Celia, near stone pedestals that were tan. They stood at the tip of the stair holding the table for the leaders. Dragons are known for their great vision, underwater and on land, and Phoenix's have great hearing. This allowed Grastem to both see and hear their conversation.

Salomne was telling Celia she had nothing to fear. The brothers had joined him in protecting her. Celia was grateful, but was no fool. She knew that her vision would still come true. There was nothing that could stop it from happening. Devoted, Salomne reassured her that nothing would happen to her. Celia then lifted her body on her toes and gave Salomne a kiss. It wasn't a long kiss, but Salomne knew it would last forever. He blushed and bowed, holding his hand out. "May I have this dance, it might help take our mind off things," he suggested.

"Yes you may," she replied.

Grastem stopped listening, all he could hear after that was the sound of their wet kiss. He found that disgusting. He turned back to Hans and Drina. He told them that he wanted to go dance the night away. Hans asked what they still were doing standing around. They all make their way to the bonfire, where the dance floor was, and danced with the heat from the flames.

CHAPTER 12

THE BURNING STAR

A N HOUR HAD gone by and Rozel has yet to find the Burning Star. He thought that when he passed the gravitational pull of Spascic's Orbit it would be right there, gliding through space. Rozel, being naive, thought it would be easy to depict. He was surrounded by a dark purple space lit up by the blue stars. Colors of purple, amber, red, and blue stretched across and exfoliated the distance. Like a milky way. There were so many stars in the galaxy; he couldn't find the specific one. Rozel was beginning to lose hope.

In the distance, he notices a sphere glowing bright. It was in the west of Spascic where he looks out for the star, but Rozel felt it couldn't have been the Burning Star.

It looked more like another planet, small like a meteor but rocks orbited around it. *How could this star have its own orbit?* He asked himself.

Rozel flew closer to get a better look. But the closer he went the brighter it became. Squinting harder the more he flew.

Rozel noticed that the sun had a lot of its light shining on it and realized that the sun may be allowing the planet to shine so bright. Stars usually shine themselves, but this one seemed to be absorbing the suns light. It wasn't hard to miss from the darkness in the galaxy.

He was getting anxious, feeling more excited the closer he got. He could feel his heart beat, pounding through his chest like a drum.

His family crossed his mind. How happy they would be that Rozel discovered another phigon. The more the thoughts ran through his mind the more it urged him to continue.

The light was burning his eyes; he used his wings to shield them.

Rozel was so distracted by his thoughts, it didn't register that he was being pulled in by the orbit's gravity until he hit the atmosphere. His Phigon body wasn't able to catch the wind under his wings. His body went into shock.

He unable to scream because of the wind choking him. He was moving so fast. Rozel looked down and saw a layer of plumped white clouds gliding through the sky. Each on followed the next, passing by. The cloud began to grow the more Rozel was falling.

Zooming past the clouds, he got soaked from the icy cold water the clouds were holding.

Snow was raining down.

As he was falling, the snow began to chase him. He was whipping through the air spiraling down, still paralyzed, unable to move.

When he landed on the ground, he smashed into it like a meteorite; crushing through the unidentified earth's crust.

He hit the ground so hard, he lost control of his phigon form and began rolling through snow.

He found his balance, and stood up. Within seconds his body began healing itself.

He brushed the snow off the remaining clothes he had on. Most of it was burned from the friction he picked up while falling.

Looking around, there was nothing but pure white snow. The snow was reflecting the sun's light off it making it hard to see. He had made it to the Burning Star.

CHAPTER 13

JIG IS UP

T HE NIGHT WAS still young. The festival had still been going on. Ithilia and Baggasin were beginning to notice that Rozel was still not seen. Myosin was sitting in her chair on the podium. Everyone else had been dancing or socializing. The two hour time limit was up for Rozel, which made Myosin annoyed and worried. Grastem noticed something was troubling her. He decided to stop dancing with his friends and go check on her.

While Grastem was making his way to her, he saw a young guy, about 18, approaching Myosin. He stopped to listen in.

"Fun festival, don't you think?" the boy said in an obviously flirtatious tone.

"Not something I like to do, but when your family is royalty, you are forced to attend these things." she replied.

"I wouldn't know anything about that. You know the royalty thing. But what do you like to do?" he asked.

Myosin had a lot on her mind. She noticed the boy's unabashed flirting. She turned to him, "Burn things. Set things on fire. Seeing the flames grow to consume its victim then diminishes." She chuckled. "That's always a fun sight to see," Her tone of voice got high, mimicking his question, 'don't you think' in a sarcastic manner.

The boy felt so uncomfortable. "Oh yeah. That sounds like a blast… literally. But um, actually, I should get back to the festivities, please excuse me." He turned away and scurried off. He was turned off by her response.

she watched him run like a girl running away from a predator, "Yeah you should."

Myosin picked up her cup of red wine made from dragons fruit, and swished it around.

Witnessing everything that just occurred, Grastem walked up to talk to Myosin and sat next to her. Grastem's chair was right in between Myosin and Salomne. Their chairs were set up was by their age. Pulling the chair up, he positioned his body forward, looking out seeing the festivities. Myosin had her hands under her chin, slouching forward looking into space.

"He was a cute boy," Grastem said.

Myosin started to sit up. She blew her breath out and words followed, "Didn't know you had eyes for girls, pixie dust," a nickname she gave Grastem. She put her elbows on the table and laid her hands down, pushing her shoulder up.

"That was a guy, Mye. He was cute for you, not for me." Grastem rolled his eyes and gave sass.

"The way he came off, I couldn't tell what his gender was." Myosin reached for her cup and swished her wine around once more. She looked at Grastem. "It's nice to know that you prefer the stem rather than the petals." She took a sip from her cup, still looking at Grastem.

Grastem laughed as if the comment didn't bother him.

"Plus, that was one of those feminine fairies, an obvious pretty boy."

"He was definitely not my type. If I wanted a guy that feminine I would date a girl, and I'm definitely not..." Myosin looked at Grastem. "Sorry, I don't mean anything by that"

Grastem's head was faced down looking at the table. He pushed his glasses up and looked at Myosin. "Have you seen Roze? Last I seen him he was with you," he asked, ignoring her comment.

"No clue," she said as she put her cup down. "He said he was going to Fairold to visit his best friend, what was his name..." She was snapping her fingers looking out into the distance. "Oh yeah. Jezzy."

Grastem was confused, he had just seen Jezzy on the dance floor, and Rozel was not with him. Grastem's no fool, he knew something was up.

"What are you hiding, Rozel isn't with Jezzy," Grastem stated.

"And how would you know that?" Myosin said confidently.

"Because he is right there," he said and pointed in Jezzy's direction. "Rozel is not with him." Grastem had caught her in her lie. "Where is Rozel?"

Myosin had given up, it had been past Rozel's time and she didn't know what else to say. She didn't want to cause a scene, so she told Grastem to keep it confidential between them. Rozel was just beginning to like Myosin and trust her, so she didn't want that to break.

Grastem started to smile.

"What are you smiling about, pixie dust?" Myosin asked.

"The fire phigon is finally showing her light. I just love it." He replied.

Grastem was happy that she was helping out his brother. Their relationship had always been on the edge ever since they were young. Myosin was the star child up until Rozel came along. They both had strong personalities.

Grastem knew that if he had told anyone, that it could ruin their relationship. Grastem promised that he would keep it confidential and would help her cover for Rozel. But if Rozel had not returned soon, he would have to alert their parents. Myosin hesitantly agreed.

Grastem didn't want her to sit here thinking about Rozel. It would make time drag. So he grabbed and pulled her onto the dance floor, and made her dance with him.

That's what she needed, someone to show her a good time. But she wasn't going to show it.

CHAPTER 14

BECOMING THE WIND

THE KING OF Spascic, Kueir, is the leader of the winged Airians.

Salomne looks up to Kueir for his victory. He hoped to be the next king after him. Being an Air Phigon, Salomne was chosen by Kueir to represent the Air Pyramids in the Andromeda. Salomne was highly honored.

Kueir had been in a tent, where he was sitting surrounded by five girls and three guys. His privacy is protected by a curtain. Two guards stand outside holding giant spears in their hands. They are wearing white chitons, and on their heads sit a gold crown molded after leaves.

Salomne spots his tent. Working up the courage, Salomne makes his way over there.

Salomne is not questioned and is able to walk in, because he is the new Airian prince.

Kueir is getting fanned by giant leaves from two women in the same chiton as the guards standing outside. Salomne notices that someone is on their knees underneath the bottom half of Kueir's chiton. Kueir doesn't tend to wear underwear because of him getting pleased often.

The girls and guys who surround him are flaunting themselves and are feeding him grapes.

"My lord." Salomne bowed as he greeted him. He was so hesitant, he felt like he was intruding.

"Ah, Salomne." Kueir was excited to see him. "Come, come. Make way, ladies and gents, your soon to be king is here." The person on their knees pulls the chiton from over their head. It was a man, blonde hair and blue eyes. He was very slim, but muscular. He was getting ready to move until Kueir stopped him and gestured him to keep going.

Salomne makes his way to find a seat next to Kueir. "Thank you." He said. Trying to avoid stepping on the man pleasing Kueir.

Kueir is a very handsome man. He's pale white, with full red lips. His hair is black and his eyes are bright blue. He is tall about 6'3 and very muscular. His wings are big and pure white. Anyone would be attracted to him.

"So, what brings you here Salomne?" Kueir asked.

Salomne didn't know what to say. He was so distracted by the man pleasuring Kueir. His eyes were glued.

Kueir snapped his fingers and nodded his head. One of the girls sitting next to Salomne began to kiss his neck. Salomne started to blush. The man pleasing Kueir had come up from under his chiton and look into Salomne's eyes. His eyes were seducing him. The man slid over towards him, not breaking his eye contact. He grabbed Salomne's crotch.

He was making Salomne aroused.

"I can't, I'm kind of seeing someone." Salomne moved the man's hand away. "I wanted to know when I will Airians start to consider me as an Airian. A lot of them have been giving me the cold shoulder. I don't think they appreciate that I am a phigon representing their nation." His toned grew strong, "I am coming to you, asking when can I start to learn the ways of the Airians?" His head bowed as he talked with honor.

Kueir looked over at him. His bright blue eyes pierce through Salomne's soul. He scooted closer into his area. "When you begin to let yourself go." His words were alluring. "Lesson number 1, let yourself be free like the wind. The wind does not care about how the water flows or how the fire burns. It doesn't even care about which direction it flows." His eye contact was keen, he grabbed Salomne's chin and lifted closer to his lips. "Don't worry about what anyone thinks. That's the truth to be an Airian. Not everyone in the Air Pyramids lives to be an Airian." Kueir answered. "You say you are 'kind of talking' but kind of talking and dating are two different things. You are still obligated to have fun." He knew he was getting through. "You want to know the ways of my people? You want to become one of us? Well it starts with letting yourself be free. Vulnerable, but not weak…" he was rubbing Salomne's upper body. He was unbuttoning his shirt, making his way down to his tight pants. He could feel that Salomne was still aroused. Salomne was falling for his seduction, his eyes had begun rolling to the back of his head. You could hear his breath moan out of his mouth. But the Kueir stopped, "and then…" Kueir suddenly said. He lifted his hands in the air, silently commanding everyone to stop. "…And only then you will become one of us."

Kueir laid back in his original spot and continued to let the man pleasure him. Salomne was stunned. His mind was racing. He never felt that before. The will to be free. He had got up, zipping his pants. His arousal had gone down. He walked out of the tent, questioning himself. He wanted more answers and knew he was the only one who could answer them.

The man lifted the chiton from over his head, "Sir, why did you let him leave? He was cute and he seemed interested," he asked.

Kueir raised his hands behind his head. His posture was cocky. "He will be back. He is the Air Phigon, it's in his blood to want freedom. We will see him again."

CHAPTER 15

THE ICE KINGDOM

ROZEL IS WANDERING around. The snow falling blinds his view in the distance. The cold air was seeping through his coat. The wind howled viciously through his ears. The noise impaired him from hearing the crunches in the snow.

In the distance, a black form appeared. It was hard to make out. It stood tall and had a dark opening. With no hesitation Rozel ran towards it. Rozel's eyes were squinting, trying to make out what it could be.

When he got closer, it was dark. The roaring of the winds still echoed. He was standing at the mouth. Concerned, he screamed hello. The cave echoed back his own voice. He stood in the cave, he could see icicles hung from the ceiling. Looking out of the cave, it was déjà vu. He had seen the same setting in his dream. His eyes were wandering, scouting out looking for any other clues. But the blizzard had been blocking his view.

He turned around and looked in the cave, he couldn't see anything.

He remembered a saying Ithilia always use to say, "There is always something at the end of a tunnel." That encouraged Rozel to search the cave. There was no wood or anything dry visible. So he had to use his senses. He started to walk.

Rozel's hands were out, he was using them as his eyes. Searching for something to stumble across, he was slipping on ice and stepping on icicles. He was at his most vulnerable moment. His dream came across his mind, remembering the ice burning him. His hands were kept straight avoiding contact with the walls.

After a while, he noticed a glowing light dimming in and out. He started to run. He had stumbled upon a door. It was glowing blue and white. It was covered in snow and completely made of ice. Rozel kicked it, only chipping it. He knew the door was thick. He used water bending to try and open it, but the door was sealed shut.

Rozel had lost hope. Just when he thought he had made some type of discovery he was shut out by a door. Rozel fell to the ground in defeat. He was holding onto his knees, breathing on them to keep him warm and waiting until the blizzard had let up before taking off back to Spascic.

Suddenly, the ground started to shake.

He saw the rocks and snow on the ground bounce from the vibrations. He looked up and noticed the door moving. Creaking as it opened. Fog came out lying across the floor.

Rozel looked up. Out walked a tall man, his skin was dark but his eyes glowed blue.

He was blind. Rozel was captivated by what he was seeing.

"Who are you?" the man asked, turning his ears in the direction of Rozel. He was barefoot, but his feet were spotless. "Where did you come from?" his voice grew.

Rozel was so enticed at his sight, he was speechless.

He started to make out words; "I" only came out as he cleared his throat. He stood up and stood in his position. "My name is Rozel, son of Ithilia and Baggasin, Leaders of the Atlantic Nation and Volcanic Tribe. I am representing the Atlantic Tribe in the next Andromeda…" He bowed. "May I ask who you might be?"

The man just stood, he didn't make a sound. Rozel looked up waiting for his answer.

"Why did you come here?" he said.

"Well I……" Rozel's voice changed. He felt intimidated.

He tried to work up the courage to speak. "I wanted to find someone by the name of Xui, he has been haunting my dreams for years now, and I think he needs my help. He is the Ice Phigon and has gone missing. Do you know where I may find him?"

The man laughed. He wasn't looking in the direction of Rozel, he was facing the wall.

His arms went up. "You're looking at him." He said giggling. "I can see you're not that smart. The clues are right in front of your face…"

He turned away and went through the doors. Rozel was still standing mesmerized at his discovery.

"Are you coming?" he said.

"Uh," he snapped out, "yes." Rozel cracked a smile, and started running behind Xui.

"Be sure not to touch the walls. The ice is very cold, it may burn your skin." he laughed as he continued to walk.

"I figured that." Rozel laughed as he chased after him.

CHAPTER 16

NEED MORE TIME

SEVERAL HOURS HAVE passed and Ithilia was worried that Rozel's outburst would stop him from showing. She was standing next to Baggasin, as he talked to his friends, she was holding a glass of wine in her hand. Her eyes were wandering, looking for Myosin. She was the last person who had seen Rozel before he took off. Instead of spotting Myosin she had seen one of the guards that had stood outside the room during her conversation with Myosin. She asked Baggasin to hold her drink.

Ithilia pulled the guard to the side, she was expressing that she hasn't seen Rozel at all that night. The guard told her that she overheard Myosin and him talking in her room. They were talking about the burning star, and how Rozel wanted to go find it. Ithilia was frustrated. She questioned the guard. *why this was the first time she was hearing this?*

Myosin had spotted him outside of her room and told the guard that Rozel was bluffing. He didn't have the courage to go. The guard didn't think anything of it once she told him that.

Ithilia was confused.

The dreams he was having were causing his curiosity to soar. Knowing Rozel for being naive, Ithilia ordered the guard to take a few troops and head out to the Burning Star. Search and bring Rozel home.

During their conversation, Myosin brushed past them. "Uh, Myosin." Ithilia grabbed her shoulder. "Have you seen your brother Rozel?"

Myosin shrugged her shoulders, "Nope." and turned away. Ithilia stepped in front, blocking her from leaving.

"Where is your brother?" She demanded.

"Nothing is going on, Mother. Rozel stormed off, he said he was headed to Fairold."

"Why is he so concerned with the Burning Star? Is it because of the dreams he's been having?"

Her eyes rolled. "Mother, I don't know. Rozel is a curious little thing."

"Myosin, if something is up you need to tell me... everything." said Ithilia.

Myosin began getting nervous. "I am telling you all that I know. It isn't much. He went off to Fairold. That was the last I saw of him." Rozel was taking up too much time and Myosin didn't know what else to say to defend him.

Myosin walked away thinking of a plan to buy more time.

She didn't want any negative thoughts running through her mind. But Rozel being hurt was all that was on her mind. She knew that everything would fall back on her. The family already thinks Rozel shouldn't hang around her because Myosin doesn't know how to stay out of trouble.

Myosin looked around for anything that could buy her time. She spotted a tree. It was in the left end of all the festivities. Lights wrapped around it for decoration.

She had the idea to burn it down. That would distract everyone, and take Ithilia's mind off Rozel.

She shot a flame through her fingertips hoping it would ignite the tree, and it burst into flames. The civilians were in a panic. Myosin grinned as she looked around to see everyone scurried around.

Grastem ran up to her. "Myosin! Why did you do this?!" he said panting.

"I'm buying Rozel more time. And how are you always able to see what I'm doing, are those glasses prescribed only to watch me?" Myosin replied.

"You plan on buying him more time by igniting the Festival Tree?! You couldn't have found a different way to buy him some time? People think they are under attack!" Grastem looked over at the tree.

Ashes were gliding in the sky.

"Well if I'm being honest here... I did this for my own amusement. I wasn't having any fun and I had to spark things up," she chuckled, "Literally."

Grastem was speechless. He looked at Myosin and just turned away. The leaders of Spascic ordered everyone remain calm. They were devising a plan to put out the tree. The Atlantic Nation gathered water from a nearby lake, Grastem used his earth ability to create boulders to surround the perimeter of the tree. But the flames were burning tall. The embers jumped off and caught onto patch of plants, causing another fire to start. It wasn't going down without a fight.

CHAPTER 17

THE BLIND ONE

ROZEL HAD ENTERED the home that belonged to Xui. He had decorated the cave into a living space using his ice ability.

There were some puddles of snow in the corners of the floors. The ceiling had a hole in it, allowing the light to come in and shine throughout his home.

Rozel couldn't feel his fingertips; they had been numb from the cold. In the center of the cave was a homemade fireplace. Xui had grabbed stick off of his counter he made and started a fire.

"Usually I only use fire for cooking. But hearing your teeth chatter is annoying me." Xui said.

Rozel was watching the way the man was walking. Every step he took, his feet made ice shards appear. His foot landed in it, crunching the ice and breaking it.

Xui pointed towards a log that sat right in front of the fireplace. "Sit there." He said. "You should get warm before you freeze to death." He went over to his bed, grabbed a blanket and handed it to Rozel.

Rozel sat down and looked at the fire. "Thank you," he said grasping the blanket. "How are you able to sustain the coldness?" he asked snuggling himself in the blanket.

"The cold has never bothered me. I created the blizzard outside; most of the snow you see came from me."

Xui made his way to the kitchen. "You must be hungry." He said reaching for a pot. He was searching in a bag that had been on the floor. Rozel hoped that whatever came out that bag was fresh.

Still sitting at the fireplace, Rozel was trying to get warm. He wondered if Xui had found what he was looking for.

Xui started walking back towards the fire; he had two bowls in his hand. He handed Rozel one of the bowls, and made his way to another log and sat across from Rozel.

Xui put the pot over the fire for a few minutes and poured a creamy liquid in his bowl, then poured some into Rozel's.

Rozel took a sip of what appeared to be soup and it electrified his body.

"Wow." The soup was spicy. It warmed him up faster than the blanket was. "This soup is amazing! What is it?"

"It's one of my grandmother's recipes. It's called Phoenix Tail Soup." He took a sip of it and smacked his mouth. "Ahh…." It sounded as if he was popping gum.

Rozel spit the soup out when he had heard the name, "Phoenix Tail?!" coughing out the words.

Xui laughed. "It's not made out of Phoenix Tails, crazy," he said. "It's called that because it reminds people of how hot a Phoenix tail actually is."

Rozel laughed as he was being corrected. "Sorry, Sir."

"Sir?" The man stopped and looked at Rozel. "I'm only twenty-one, there's no need to call me that."

"Twenty-one?" Rozel questioned.

"Well two hundred and ten in dragon years but twenty-one is a lot shorter to say," he said.

"Understood." Rozel took another sip of his soup. "So you are Xui?" Rozel looked over at him swishing around his bowl.

Xui looked up at Rozel; he had pronounced his name wrong as if he said Zay.

"Zu-ay, Xui... My name is Xui." His eyes were scouting out Rozel's area.

Rozel's voice lit up with cheer. "I am so honored to meet you!" He said, ecstatically setting his bowl down. He clenched onto the blanket around him and jumped up, to bow.

"Watch the bowl; these are the only ones I have." Xui said. "What of my name?! Why are you bowing?" Xui had sensed his movements.

"You can see me? I thought..." Rozel was fascinated.

"Yeah, yeah I'm blind. But I can still see you." Xui said pointing his finger like an elderly women.

"I didn't mean to offend you, I was trying to avoid... Forget it, you're Xui! I've been searching for you!" Rozel sat back down. "You're a Phigon like me!" Rozel was pointing at himself.

"Impossible..." Xui was confused. "My father killed them all in a massacre." The memory caused his voice to dim, "It was genocide."

"It's true! I'm a Phigon. So are my brothers Salomne, and Grastem and my sister, Myosin."

"There are four of you?" Xui stood up. He walked over to Rozel and sat next to him. He grabbed his face and skimmed it with fingers. He was shocked. "It's true."

Rozel was gazing into his eyes; he didn't know how he was able to tell. He pulled his hand down from his face. "Yes, it is and I came here to ask you, why I might be having dreams about you?"

Xui was taken back. "Dreams about me? I have no idea… Wish I could help you." He got up and walked back to the other log across from Rozel. "To be honest, I'd thought no one would remember me after all this time. I've been trapped here for almost ten years."

"That's just it. No one knows of your existence. I've been having recurring dreams about you."

Xui had been confused. "In these dreams, what were you doing? What was I doing?" Xui asked.

"We were in a cave similar to one we are in. You didn't know I was there." Rozel explained, "I'm not sure if you were running away or running towards something but I was following you." Xui's face shot up. He got up and started walking to the other log. Rozel looked at him cautiously and continued, "When you made it out the cave you ran to a tombstone made of Ice. In the last dream I fell, which caused you to look over at me. You then whirled up a wind of snow, and vanished. I couldn't believe my eyes."

Xui put his head on his hand. He was distraught. "It was you!" He was looking at his feet scrunching the dirt in his toes. "I knew I felt someone here…" he looked up at Rozel, "I was running away from you." His voice sounded relieved. "You've been astral projecting. Your spirit had wandered here." He smiled and looked into the fire. His voice had calmed down from excitement. "I thought I had been founded by the people who were trying to kill me."

"Who are they?" Rozel questioned.

"Subjeckies. Phoenix troops who follow my father Wetchador. They are against anything that isn't the phoenix way. Just like my father. They are the ones who wiped out the phigons who were alive. But it didn't stop there; they killed anyone who was gay because it wasn't normal to be that way, anyone disabled because he saw them to be weak, anyone of color was banned from touching the grounds of the Volcanic Tribe. That is until he met the mother of Dragons, Flocean." Xui had still been staring into the fire. "He wanted my brother and I, dead. The only two kids he ever had." His voice was fading.

Rozel chimed in to share his research. "Zender. Right? The Lightning Phigon... It's incredible. You guys had remarkable abilities." Rozel was looking at Xui stare into the fire.

Xui looked past the fire at Rozel. "How do you know so much about me? For someone who is so curious, you seem to know everything."

Rozel snapped out of his amazement and caught onto Xui's sarcasm. "Uh, well I actually looked you up in the book of ancestors me and my sister Myosin found using the legend of scrolls. It showed me that a woman by the name of Myrtle Merlow rescued you from your father's reign and kept you alive."

"Rescued?" His voice fell into a mumble. "More like captured." He looked back into the fire.

"Captured? I thought she helped you escape your father. He killed Zender and just before he got you, Myrtle saved you."

"That mustn't be the right history book if it tells you that," he said, chuckling. "Myrtle didn't save me. She kidnapped me. I think about that day all the time." Xui got up. He had walked over to his bed. He got on his knees and felt underneath it.

He pulled out a bag.

Coming to his feet, Xui shook the bag up and down. It sounded like marbles rattling. He reached in and pulled a handful of colorful beads, handing them to Rozel. "I will show you what truly happened."

He pulled out a purple bead and held it up. "These are Magi Beads. Each colorful bead I pull out, you must find the matching color and throw it into the fire with me. When inhaled the fire's smoke, it will allow you to see the visions in my head."

Rozel fondled the beads.

Scattering through the bag, he found a matching purple one. Xui slammed the bead down shattering it. Purple sand spilled on the ground.

Dust sparkled around.

Xui shuffled his feet around the sand, inhaling.

He positioned on the floor, beginning to meditate.

Rozel was fascinated; he noticed Xui pressing down on the sand.

Rozel threw the bead into the fire.

An exploding sound echoed off the cave walls. The fire had turned purple and the glitter was burning. Each one snapping as the fire devoured it. The smoke had become purple and transparent. Rozel looked up at the sight, he was star-struck. Rozel followed Xui and closed his eyes to meditate. Hoping that's what Xui wanted him to do.

The moon's light entered the hole in the ceiling; shining on them. Suddenly their eyes shot open. They were white, glowing like the moonlight. Their heads began to face up as if they were possessed. Their eyes shot a beam of light out into the sky. Their minds were now linking.

CHAPTER 18

VISIONS OF THE PAST

R OZEL'S SOUL HAD landed into a dark area. He didn't know where he was. His body was left in front of the fire. Rozel looked behind and saw Xui was sitting on the floor. He was still meditating. A voice appeared; it was Xui's. When Rozel looked over at him Xui, his mouth was shut. He was speaking through his mind. Rozel began to worry. He called out for Xui. But he remained still. Xui had told Rozel to sit down and remain calm.

A vision appeared. It formed like the Northern Lights across the darkness. Xui's voice echoed, "This is what truly happened: *Twelve years had passed since we were born. My brother and I trained every day. My father knew his time* would come to an end as ruler but he wanted to make sure that his reign wouldn't."

Rozel could believe what he was seeing.

"He wasn't aware of the power we possessed until this day." A vision was shown of them training. "When we finally realized our true gifts, the world began to worship us. The other phigons didn't have the elemental gifts me and my brother had. No one had seen the power Zender and I had. Ice and Lightning coming from phigons was the rarest thing.

The leaders of each nation wanted one of us to represent them in the next Andromeda. I had gone with representing the Atlantic Nation and Zender chose to go with the Air Pyramids. I went with whatever I saw as a better chance at winning and becoming the new leader. I wanted to change the world.

When Wetchador was made aware of our choices, he was infuriated. He had thought that our power belonged to him. He couldn't believe neither of us wanted to represent the Volcanic Tribe."

The visions had changed to a coliseum. It showed Zender and Xui standing in front of each other. "Jealous grew and it enraged my father. He ordered me and Zender to fight in front of the world of Spascic. This was where the Andromeda takes place. He felt that since we were old enough to make choice of who we wanted to represent, we were old enough to battle each other.

Wetchador sat on a ledge overseeing everything, smiling upon his children fighting. Zender gave it all he had, without holding back. He wanted to get away from father, and winning the battle would make sure of that. Bolts of lightning were striking at me. I dodged them by forming objects made of ice to shield myself. I used the best of my ability to attack him. We weren't brothers in that ring.

I could tell Wetchador wasn't feeling amused after we were showcasing our power because his cheering had faded. He leaned over the balcony and focused on our techniques.

In the midst of us battling, he called out for us to stop. He jumped down off the ledge, ripping his cape and shirt off. Wetchador wanted to take us both on. The crowd roared as they cheered the battle on. It was us against our father.

The battle was lasting for hours and there was no holding back. We may have been phigons but my father's power nearly matched. He was incredible. I knew, from that battle, I wanted to be King more than anything.

I put the most energy and effort that was possible.

My ice powers were weak against his blaze but I was not giving up. He took us both on like we were nothing. He barely broke a sweat.

Zender and I had to think of something quick. We were losing stamina, slowly trying to keep up. Wetchador caught on to us becoming weak and took advantage. He blasted Zender, it was like a bullet piercing the through the air and then exploding as it hit its target. I've seen this before. Wetchador was trying to kill Zender.

I had become scared. The thought of losing my brother broke me. I shifted into my phigon, causing a blizzard to form. The crowd was shocked. Wetchador turned into a Phoenix. The wind was so cold Wetchador's flames weren't showing. He screeched out to the sky like a hawks calling, and transformed back into a human. He accepted his defeat. When I had turned back, Wetchador hugged me and declared me heir to the throne. Everyone shouted my name, praising me. But I could see in his eyes that he was still envious.

Later that night, I was awoken by the screams and cries of civilians. Flames were touching the sky; burning houses and villages. My mother stormed in the room Zender and I was in. She said that we needed to go. She had bruises on her arms and legs. Her clothes were burned. We didn't ask any questions, we just obeyed. She wrapped us in coats with hoods on them to disguise us. She flew us out to Fairold; but her dragon body didn't blend in with the flames too well. She brought us to the leader of the Fairies, Myrtle Merlow, who, at the time, had been the most powerful Fairy. We met her in a sanctuary where she practiced most of her magic. My mother asked if she could help us escape. Help create a new world for us to live on. Myrtle laughed, she said that creating a new world was way too powerful, even for her. My mother had asked if there was anything Myrtle could do. But Myrtle just laughed and kept saying that this was the bed she wanted to lay in.

Turning away, my mother held our hands and we walked out. When we had walked outside the Subjeckies had caught up to us. Most of the town was destroyed. They knew we were there and followed us. Myrtle ran outside to see the catastrophe.

The Subjeckies were surrounding us. My mother screamed out to Myrtle asking if she could take Zender and I, as she held them off.

Myrtle did so.

Zender was crying out for our mother but Myrtle had us gripped in her hands. She took us back into the sanctuary. She rambled through spells, potions, dusts, and sands; packing anything she could find. Zender's eyes were glued to the door that sealed us in. He was so concerned for our mother. I was more concerned about surviving with my brother. I knew our mother was strong enough to take them on.

Myrtle handed us a pill. She told us to take it so it would make us stronger and protect us from any harm for a while. We were so naive to believe her. Once we took it, our bodies instantly became numb. It began paralyzing our legs all the way up to our neck. I saw Zender collapse on the floor.

I got so anxious witnessing that.

I fell shortly after, my eyes blurred and I felt light headed. I saw the door burst open as flames wandered in. A form of a muscular man stood in the doorway. It was my father. I blacked out."

The visions went black. Rozel was speechless, He couldn't fathom what he was seeing.

Xui was still meditating. Another vision had come to view; it was of Xui waking up panting. Myrtle was pouring a cup of tea, waiting for him to wake from his slumber. They had been in the same cave, Rozel was in.

"She brought you here?" Rozel called out.

Xui still did not budge. The vision only showed him in the room with Myrtle.

The voice appeared. *"Myrtle had brought me here. Yes. But it was for her own personal gain. Myrtle had been creating this world for years, she lied to my mother. She was, indeed, powerful enough to create another world.*

I asked her what had happened to Zender and my mother. She told me that they both had died. Wetchador had killed them."

Rozel's eyes began to tear. Xui had been only 12 when all of this happened. He was the only one out of his family who made it alive. "You were the only one who survived," Rozel said softly.

"So I believed too. But Myrtle had a thing for lying and deceiving.

Many years had passed. I was about 15 years old. Myrtle took care of me as one of her own. Trained me, helped me control my ability. Taught me how to cook; taught me how to do some spells. She had become my new guardian." Xui's voice was calm.

"That doesn't sound so bad," Rozel called out.

"I haven't finished yet, Rozel." He said

"Things were great. I was beginning to love her as a mother.

Until I found her journal, she wrote everything in; her deepest regrets, her darkest secrets." Xui's voice turned angry. Rozel began to feel a breeze of cold air swoop in. *"Myrtle was gone. She had left to find herbs and fruits for dinner. So I had enough time to take a glimpse into her journal. I read that my mother had actually died fighting off the Subjeckies and my father. She told the truth there, but she failed to be truthful when she said my brother Zender died.*

Myrtle gave him away to Wetchador after we had passed out. They made a deal; if Myrtle can keep one of his sons, she will give him the other." His voice sounded disgusted.

"When Myrtle returned, I was sitting on my bed trying to recollect my thoughts; praying I'd find the words to what I would say. She knew something was wrong. My expression was obvious.

Myrtle came over to sit next to me, wondering why I had tears falling down my face. I held her journal up and threw it on the ground.

I asked her if it was true.

She couldn't even look me in my face. I was screaming and yelling. I felt like a fool, I created the tombstone, you had seen in your dreams, in remembrance of Zender and my mother.

I told Myrtle that I felt that my brother was still alive, but she kept reminding me that he was dead.

I told her I was going to set out to find my brother.

I started packing my things and gathering food. I was headed back to Spascic wherever it was." Xui's aura had changed. The blue light that surrounded him began to glow red.

The vision showed Myrtle still sitting there; fiddling with her hands. Xui couldn't help but to look at her in the midst of him packing.

The vision then showed Xui running out the cave. Though the tunnel was long, Xui was very fast. Thoughts of rescuing his brother helped boost his adrenaline.

"When I finally made it outside, I shifted instantly and took off; jetting through the sky." Xui's light was still glowing red. The voice echoing was becoming aggressive. The vision showed Xui abruptly stopped. *"But then my eyes started to feel so heavy. I was beginning to see nothing but a blur. Something pulled me, causing me to crash into the ground. My phigon form couldn't take it so I turned back.*

Hurt from the falling, I struggled to get up.

I ended up at the mouth of the cave. I couldn't see much, but I depicted Myrtle standing in the entrance, walking towards me. My eyes were dimming to black. I could hear her saying, 'I raised you as my son. You will not abandon me.'

A few moments later, I could not see anything. My eyesight was gone." Xui's voice diminished in the distance.

Rozel had been so engaged in the vision. "She took your eyesight and she kept you from your brother." He said.

"It wasn't just that, she took my freedom." Xui called out.

"What happened to her?" Rozel asked.

"As angry as I was, I knew I was too vulnerable to attack her. So I plotted my revenge for the perfect moment. Years had passed and Myrtle did not train me anymore. We were hardly speaking.

So I trained myself. The ice shards you see me create to take a step, allow me to see with my feet. I learned that by me cracking the ice with my feet, it allows me to hear the vibrations and see the sound waves to depict out an object, resulting in me seeing with my feet.

Once I got the hang of things, I knew that I needed to act on my revenge.

One night I was walking back into the cave, Myrtle noticed the ice I was using to step on. I didn't give her the chance to speak. I just sensed her standing in front of me. I created a million of sharp icicles that covered the ceiling. She tried to dodge them as they fell but she couldn't avoid it. The icicles pierced through her body and through her skull, killing her.

Now ever since then, I've been stuck here praying to the Gods that I find my way out. I still have the feeling Zender is alive, but after all these years I have been losing hope in finding him."

The visions and dimmed and Xui's body had stopped glowing. They had begun regaining consciousness. The light that shot up to the moon had shot back down into their bodies.

When Rozel had awoken, he noticed himself moving. It was a dark area. Rozel started to blink, thinking it he was still in his state of consciousness, but he was not.

Xui was lying next to him, as his eyes began to open.

Rozel felt around and noticed they were in a confined metal box. Scared, Rozel started to panic. He banged on the metal walls that surrounded him. Xui was unaware of his surroundings. He kept asking Rozel what was going on but Rozel did not listen and continued to bang.

"Rozel!" Xui grabbed onto him and pulled him down. "What is going on?!"

"We are trapped! In metal box! I can't see anything, everything is dark, I'm scared."

"Well welcome to the dark side where everything is dark because you know, you can't see." Xui was being sarcastic. "I knew this day would come… At least I'm not stuck on that world anymore." Xui threw his arms up.

Rozel was confused. He didn't know what Xui meant by him knowing this day would come. He had no idea where he was going.

CHAPTER 19

CAPTURED

SEVERAL HOURS HAD passed after the festival clean-up from the fire.

Rozel still hadn't come back yet.

Ithilia's heart was crushed. She was sitting in front of a mirror, as a young girl brushed her hair. She wasn't looking at her reflection; her head was down and pressed on her hand.

She was waiting on a response from the men she sent to find Rozel. Hoping they would return with good news. She tried to keep a positive mind, but so many questions were running through.

Then she remembered Myosin trying to avoid telling her about Rozel's disappearance. Ithilia sat up had told the young girl to go fetch Myosin from her room. She had no desire to play any games with Myosin. It had already been midnight and Rozel was still not found. The guards were still searching for him.

When Myosin entered, Ithilia ordered everyone to leave. She wanted to have the room with herself and her daughter.

"Myosin," she said as she got up from the chair in front of her mirror, "where is Rozel?" Her left hand was placed on top of her right hand. She was slowly walking towards Myosin, scarcely.

Myosin's guilt had been eating away at her. Rozel was her responsibility and she still hadn't heard a word from him. She knew she couldn't hold the truth back from her mother anymore. So she confessed, "He is at the Burning Star…"

"The Burning Star?! He is alone, outside of this world!?" Ithilia screamed.

"Yes." Myosin's voice was soft. "He went there to go find the guy who he was dreaming about."

"Why would he go to the Burning Star for that?!" Ithilia asked.

"We read it in the Shakawa. The guys name is Xui. He vanished a long time ago with a woman by the name Myrtle Merlow."

"Xui? Myrtle!" Her eyes glistened with tears. "How...? Why didn't you tell me any of this?!"

Myosin was hesitant to answer, "Rozel thought he could do it all on his own. After the fight you guys had, he knew he wouldn't get this opportunity again, so I helped cover for him," Myosin pleaded. "Please don't be mad at me, I just wanted to help my brother out. We usually don't get along and we finally found something we both were passionate about." Myosin was trying to manipulate the situation.

There was a knock on the door.

"Go away!" yelled Ithilia.

"But your highness, I have returned from the burning star. I have news." A voice said through the cracked door.

"Come in," Ithilia said eagerly. "What's the news?!" she said whipping the door open.

A guard who was very tall and hefty made his way into the room. You couldn't see his lips because his beard blocked them. "Madam, when the troops and I went to venture off to the Burning Star, a light glowed coming from the star. The light was connecting to the moon. But by the time we made it there, it had faded away." His beard moved up and down, like a lumberjack talking.

Myosin could help but laugh. But Ithilia silenced her immediately. It was no laughing matter.

She ordered the guard to continue.

"The Burning Star is a world not a star. It literally was bright because of the snow reflecting the suns light. We tried to investigate as much as we could. But most of the world was burning from flames." The man handed her a burnt rugged cloth, "We were only able to find this."

It had a symbol of a golden Phoenix.

Ithilia's eyes opened wide. Her voice growled, "Call Baggasin… NOW!"

The guard ran off and sounded the alarm. Ithilia turned away making her way back to her chair.

Myosin ran up to her. "Mom, what is it?"

Ithilia clenched onto the cloth and held it against her heart. "Rozel was captured."

"By whom, Mother?" asked Myosin.

"Subjeckies," she mumbled in fear.

Ithilia slowly set the cloth down in front of the mirror and walked out of the room. Myosin was scared. She didn't know what was going to happen to Rozel. But she was more afraid of what her punishment would be rather than Rozel's condition.

CHAPTER 20

PANIC

T HE SIRENS SILENCED.
Ithilia made her way down the hall; Baggasin
had been running up the stairs.

In his face, you could tell his panic. Baggasin knew
that Rozel had been missing from the festival but thought
nothing of it. Due to the fight, he had with Ithilia, he
wanted to give Rozel some space.

With Rozel being gone for hours, Baggasin couldn't
help but to think the worst.

"Ithilia, what happened?" He asked.

He had made it to the top of the stair. Ithilia fell into
his arms. Baggasin was expecting tears, but he instead
got an aggressive response.

"Myosin let him fly off to the Burning Star, which turns out to be an actual world. He was looking for the man in his dreams." Ithilia's tone was anxious.

Myosin ran up after her. She was trying to explain herself but Baggasin silenced her. "Myosin, why would you let your brother fly off by himself?" He let go of Ithilia and faced Myosin. He was trying to retrain himself. Ever since he slapped Myosin for burning Rozel, he felt guilty and tried anything to make up for it.

Myosin didn't back down. She stood tall, expressing Rozel's request to go by himself. At this point, she was getting annoyed with her parents. She didn't care if everything fell back on her but Rozel was his own person, and could make his own decisions.

Rozel was the youngest and the most gullible but she didn't feel bad for not going with him. It was something he needed to do on his own. Myosin felt she was helping him grow up.

Salomne and Grastem ran in through the entrance of their castle. They thought the sirens rang for them to come back home.

Grastem saw Myosin at the top of the stairs, facing Baggasin. Unaware of what was going on, he quickly made his way to the top of the stairs; he was ready to rescue Myosin from whatever trouble she got herself into.

Salomne followed after, he had an announcement he was ready to share, "Mother, Father." he bowed to them. He didn't acknowledge Myosin. "I have great news. I will be leaving tonight. I am going to the Air temple to train and work on myself. The Airians are going to help cleanse my mind, which should help me with my air bending."

"Tonight?" Ithilia asked. It wasn't a good time for him to leave.

"Yes, the Andromeda is right around the corner and we should all set out and begin our training."

"Wouldn't that be lovely," Myosin smiled sarcastically, "but unfortunately our dearest brother is missing," She started taking shots at him, "But it's okay, I know your brain tends to soar with the wind so you probably haven't realized it yet, or even cared."

Salomne didn't respond. A part of him felt that Myosin was telling the truth but he didn't want to give her the satisfaction. He turned to Ithilia, "Mother, is this true?" he asked.

"Sadly," she said devastated. "Myosin let him run off to find the man in his dreams. Myosin says his name is Xui."

Baggasin looked at her. The name struck him. Ithilia nodded her head at him. They knew exactly who Xui was.

Baggasin said concerned, "But he died, they all did."

"So I thought too. I have a cloth that was left on the planet. It had a golden Phoenix on it. Anything else was burning from flames." Ithilia was giving hints.

"You don't think…" Baggasin said.

"Yes, subjeckies." Ithilia had tears in her voice. "They could have captured him or killed him. Who knows? He's a Phigon."

"What are Subjeckies? Who took him?!" Grastem yelled.

"They are troops of your mother's father, Wetchador. When we were little, they used a symbol a golden Phoenix signifying Wetchador being The Phoenix Emperor," Baggasin replied. "I thought they had vanished after he lost his power, but I guess not." Baggasin was trying to put the pieces together.

"We have to do something! Where could he be?" Salomne asked.

"Shouldn't you be packing for feather dusting school?" Myosin chuckled.

"Silence yourself! You're the reason we are all in this mess. Rozel's death is on your hands!" Salomne answered.

"No," Grastem chimed in. "You should go." Everyone stopped and looked at him as if he was crazy. "You shouldn't think the worst of things..." Grastem looked at Myosin, "You are right. This is Myosin's mess, she needs to clean it. And I'll help her. You should go train." Grastem smiled and touched salmon shoulder.

"Wait, are you sure?" Salomne asked hesitant.

"Positive. We will be fine. Two of the most powerful Phigons? I would be afraid of us. Right?" Grastem nudged Myosin with his elbow. Myosin looked unsure. She didn't know where Grastem was getting at.

"Alright, I trust you Grastem," Salomne said.

"Not so fast," Ithilia stepped in, "What are your plans to rescue him, What if you guys get captured too?!"

"Don't worry too much, Ithilia. I believe they are smart enough to handle themselves," Baggasin said looking into Grastem's eyes. He could sense his determination.

Grastem asked to see the cloth. He had a plan to take it to Fairold.

Celia would be able to use a locator spell and find Rozel in a heartbeat. Myosin didn't know what was happening, but she had no choice but to tag along.

After Ithilia handed the cloth to Grastem, he grabbed Myosin's hand and walked to the balcony. She couldn't help but smile at Grastem, defending him. She knows she is going to pay him back, she just didn't know how yet.

They shifted into their phigons and flew out.

CHAPTER 21

GRASTEM AND MYOSIN had just arrived to a swamp outside of Fairold. If they wanted to get to the city gates, they were going to have to make it through there. Grastem's earth ability makes it easier for them to maneuver the plants out of the way.

During their walk, Grastem didn't talking. His mind wasn't on Rozel's rescue, but Salomne's departure. Salomne is supposed to be the oldest brother, protecting all of them. Yet all he cared about was training for the Andromeda.

Myosin knew something was wrong. She and Grastem have a close bond despite the remarks and antics she makes. She sensed the lack of care to rescue Rozel coming from Salomne. He was more dedicated to learning the ways to his ability than finding his brother.

"You felt it too, huh?" Myosin asked. But Grastem did not answer. He just kept walking ahead. "You know, I didn't mean for this to happen." She shrugged her shoulders, "Okay, yeah, I wanted him to get in trouble when he got home, but I honestly did want him to find what he was looking for," Myosin confessed. But still Grastem didn't respond. "I can tell you're not mad at me. You're mad at Salomne." Myosin was trying to dig, "He didn't even fight you when you told him to go."

Myosin turned her face and made her voice high and goofy. "Just a 'Are you sure', and nothing more." Her voice grew shallow, "But Everyone hates me though."

"No one hates you." Grastem finally spoke. "Disappointed, but not hate." He stopped where he was walking. "You put yourself in these terrible predicaments, but you don't think of what can happen. You never ask yourself what the outcome might be." He turned to face Myosin. "Why…? Why do you put yourself in these situations? For the attention? Because all you're getting is negative attention."

Myosin responded throwing her hands up. "The way I see it, attention is attention, even if it's bad. I have to find some way to be in the spotlight." She started to walk past. "Being good and isolating myself never got me anything but a slap in the face." Myosin didn't show any emotion. She just kept walking as Grastem followed behind her. "Everyone's seen a monster then, without me even trying, so now they got one."

"No one sees you as a monster. That's your own perception of yourself," Grastem fired back.

Myosin stopped. "Everyone does, even our mother." Myosin was speaking so calmly it was scary. She was looking in the sky noticing the tall trees blocking the sun. "Our own mother thinks I'm a monster…." She looked over to Grastem and shrugged her shoulders again. Her voice changed. She was no longer sad. "She's right of course but it still hurts me," she said confidently as she continued to walk.

Grastem knew at that moment, Myosin had emotions that she blocked from showing. "I don't hate you." Grastem said softly as he watched Myosin walk ahead. He was moving the giant roots and plants from their pathway.

"I know I tell you this every time you get me out of trouble. But I will repay you someday, Grastem. I have to expressed this to you," she said aggressively.

Myosin had a tear run down her face. Grastem didn't notice because she walked ahead of him.

The hours were passing by.

Myosin began to get frustrated. There were so many plants and flowers around her. She shot fire at them; burning them into ashes. But it was no use. The plants regenerated quickly and grew bigger. The more she burned the more they grew. Grastem warned her that if she didn't stop, the plants will over power them. The swamp was alive and so were the plants, at any time they could devour them and kill them. After a while she stopped.

Grastem walked in front of Myosin and maneuvered the plants. He didn't want Myosin's rage killing them. Grastem saw an opening in the distance.

When they made their way to it, the city gates were a few steps away.

Passing the gate would require an invitation from one of the leaders. But because Grastem will be the new leader, he and his sister were able to make it through.

They wasted no time. Finding Rozel was urgent. They made it to the sanctuary, home of the prayers that belong to the civilians of Fairold. It is called the Grass Castle.

Celia was there. She has the title of being one of the most powerful Fairies due to her gift of foreseeing future events, only the rarest fairies can do.

She was always at the grass castle, praying about the sights she had seen or were going to see.

Outside were two tanned, muscular guards who wore grass skirts. Protecting the entrance.

They were standing in front of the pathway to the sanctuary; surrounded by lilies that sparkled as the light shined upon them. The wet grass glistened. The trees whistled as the birds sang. It was truly a peaceful area.

Myosin asked if they could speak to Celia; expecting a yes.

But the guard turned them both down. Even Grastem.

Myosin explained that it was no request, but a demand. Barking up a fight, Grastem stepped in to avoid any conflict between his sister.

Grastem was impatient. He conjured up stems from the ground. They wrapped around the guards' bodies, slamming them into the wall behind them. Grastem, with no hesitation stepped over the root of the stems, and began walking inside the sanctuary.

Myosin mocked the guards and laughed, as she chased after Grastem.

Celia had been kneeling in front of steps that led to a bench, holding flowers of all kinds. It represented, that they may be all different, but all the flowers need the same resources.

She had a bandeau made of flowers and a grass skirt on. A rose held her hair behind her ear. She looked in the corner of her eye, as she turned her head slightly. She was expecting them to come.

"Celia, what was that about?" Grastem asked.

"No one is to be disturbed during their prayers. It's an insult to the Gods," Celia replied.

"Listen, pixie hollow. We need you to do something," Myosin demanded.

"Locate Rozel," Celia said calmly.

"You know?" Grastem asked softly. "Where is he?"

"I am sure that Salomne has told you of my vision. The one of my death."

"And what celebration it will be at your funeral?" Myosin cheered.

Celia looked at Myosin and laughed. "Well, your brother is with that threat. They were captured by Subjeckies," Celia explained

Myosin cut her off. "Yeah, yeah. We've heard. We need to know where he is."

"Quit it." Grastem hit Myosin and began walking up to Celia. "We need to find our brother. Can you help?"

"That, I cannot." Celia said.

"Wait, Why?!" said Grastem.

"I can honestly say, that I am jealous at all the people who will never met you," Myosin said with a straight face.

Celia looked at Myosin, then turned to Grastem."As long as they are captured, I will remain alive. I have no threat."

"That threat has nothing to do with Rozel! We need to know where he is!" Grastem was becoming annoyed.

"Here's a deal. I will tell you the location of your brother's whereabouts. If you bring the ice boy to me."

"Technically he is a man. Not a boy, and apparently his name is Xui," Myosin said sarcastically.

"Shut up Mye," said Grastem. He had been getting frustrated. Grastem turned to Celia and made the deal with her. He would return Xui to her if she gave them the location.

Celia chanted one of her spells, Grastem gave her one of Rozel's shirts he brought. It didn't take long for her find the exact place they had been held. It was Far East from the Volcano in the Volcanic Tribes village. There was a secret society of phoenixes who built a city on an island. The island burned so hot some the sand turned into glass. It shined like gold. That was why the phoenixes called it the Golden Island.

The Subjeckies kept Rozel and Xui, in the most secured cage made of metal; in the center of the island. Celia warned them that it the phoenix's had great power. She couldn't explain where they had learned how to enhance their ability, but it was like no other phoenix in the Volcanic Tribe. They were going to be in for a fight.

Grastem didn't care. He took off with the information he got. Myosin was struggling to keep up with Grastem speed. They set off towards the Golden Island.

CHAPTER 22

THE WILL OF LETTING GO

WITH GRASTEM AND Myosin out looking for Rozel, Salomne had the opportunity to go out to the Air Pyramids.

It was located in the sky, sitting on clouds; directly above from the Volcanic Tribe.

Pegasus's fly around like birds in the sky, their white feathers from their wings rained over the city.

Salomne didn't alert Kueir of his visit. But Kueir had been expecting him.

Salomne thought about what happened at the festival. His mind was so focused on knowing more about the people of the Air Pyramids. He wanted to be one of them, flowing like the wind.

Anyone representing in the Andromeda has to be trained by the nation's previous leader.

Myosin will represent the Volcanic Nation. Ithilia is the new leader and will train her.

Before the genocide of all phigons, Wetchador was having a secret affair with Ithilia's mother, a phoenix named Althea. When Ithilia was 20 years old she witnessed the phigons being killed.

When his reign ended, Wetchador needed a new life. He married Althea. Ithilia became the next leader of the Volcanic Tribe and was the to fight in the Andromeda, where she met Baggasins. After Kuier won, Wetchador disappeared along with his troops. He hated idea of what the world would become.

Baggasin resigned his position as leader of the Atlantic nation after the Andromeda. He moved to the Volcanic Tribe to live with Ithilia and their children. Kidley, is now the leader of the nation and he will train Rozel.

Greta, Leader of Fairold and mother of Celia, will train Grastem.

Training takes two out of the three years. And the Andromeda was three years away.

Time is different on Spascic. Each year that passed on Spascic, meant ten years had passed on earth.

The Andromeda takes place every ten years, meaning a century has passed on earth.

Typically, each nation has a member of their race representing their own country. Now that there are phigons, a new beast that inhabits the ability of the elements, each nation has a better chance of winning.

Fairies usually use the energy magic against their opponents.

Arians, use their wings to fly and dodge attacks while shooting arrows through their bows. They rarely use other weapons like spears and shields to fight and protect, because their hard to maneuver around.

Dragons use their strength and endurance. They hide under water and use swimming as an advantage. Phoenix's use their speed and their elemental property of fire as their weapons.

Each technique is tradition that has been around for years. Every Andromeda, the competition gets greater.

Salomne is getting a head start on his training. Salomne doesn't feel threatened. His ego is high; bets are already being bided on Salomne to win.

He has studied his siblings in and out. He knows all of their strengths and weaknesses.

Grastem's ground abilities may give him a chance. But without confidence, Grastem can't win.

The city of the Airian resides in the center, surrounded by the pyramids. Flying is the only way of getting to it.

That night, Salomne makes it to Kueir Castle.

Salomne's been thinking about the temptation from Kueir's sexual attraction to him, but knew he was still with Celia.

Salomne wants to be an Airian, but knows he needs to sacrifice his relationship with Celia before he can commit. He has to learn the ways, in order to officially become the leader, and be considered an Arian.

He shifted back into himself, when he lands in front of the castle steps.

His heart was racing. The adrenaline from the other night was making him anxious for more. But he didn't want to let Celia down.

The question, what would she think of him, was running through his head. If he was to sleep with someone else out, he doesn't think she would ever forgive him. They were just starting to get serious.

The guilt was getting to him.

Salomne decided that he needed to turn back and see Celia. He couldn't go on feeling obligated to her and they weren't official.

In the past, she toyed with him and he didn't want it to happening again.

Before he could turn away a voice called out for him. "Hey Salomne!" Kueir said, "I was expecting you to show."

He had just walked out the castle with his arms open for a hug.

Kueir Pulled Salomne in. Someone had alerted him that Salomne had shown up and Kueir wanted to personally greet him.

Salomne's feelings of guilt disappeared. He felt honored by the King. Kueir hugged him passionately. Salomne embraced his tight grip.

As they let go, Kueir offered to show him around the city of the Air Pyramids.

They walked through the modernized colonies. They could see the stars up close, lighting up the night sky.

There were no bakery shops, food markets, or stands. Despite the churton they wore, everything was modern; new houses, fashion clothing stores for the churtons, regular shopping markets and even hair salons. Salomne had never seen anything like this.

"I wanted to expand my ideas around the world. But I spent most of my time as king rebuilding this new city." Kueir showed passion about his ideas as he explained. "Most of the other villages are stuck in the past. They like the idea of an old fashioned town…" They walked slow, gazing at each building they passed. "I convinced Greta to let me create a new city for the fairies, but it would take years before I could build another great city like this one. Soon I won't be king anymore." Kueir and Salomne saw more new things as they turned the corner. Kueir gave Salomne a great position. "That's why I want you to carry on my legacy."

They made it to a park. There had been swings made of puffy clouds. The sand on the ground was dark grey. The color mimicked the clouds. In the center was a Kueir statue made of gold.

They went over to the nearest bench and sat facing the statue "That will be you one day," Kueir said.

Salomne was pleased to hear the confidence Kueir had in him.

"How did you manage to defeat my parents in battle?" Salomne asked. The question had always been lingering in his head.

"It wasn't easy." He said. "I had to let go of the personal things holding me down. Break myself from the chain preventing me from flying off with the wind. I became a free spirit." Kuier laughed a little, "I had to take on Greta head on. Your mother and father battled each other. Your mother showed her true power. I think Baggasins underestimated her potential. She took him out first. I knew she was going to be a difficult opponent. She is the daughter of Wetchador of course. Greta didn't put up a fight. She was hiding from me most of the time.

When I finally found her, she threw her hands up and quit without any hesitation."

"Why did she quit?" Salomne asked.

Kueir looked into his eyes. "She was pregnant with Celia." He patted on Salomne's lap and lifted himself up. "The girl you say you are talking…" He was looking into the distance. "She will only hold you back." Kueir turned back, "You are so young." He said, "You must experience life and understand who you are first. Don't settle at the level you are on. Life has so much more to offer. Let the wind show you the way."

Salomne had thought about what he was saying. The words were so powerful.

He got up and began to walk. Kueir stood there and watch him leave. He knew where Salomne was going. He needed to clear his thoughts. His devotion to become the new leader of the air pyramids was greater than anything.

Salomne shifted into his beast and started to fly, he was heading to Fairold.

CHAPTER 23

THE GOLDEN ISLAND

ROZEL AND XUI were dragged out of the box. They tried to fight the man and woman holding them, but there bending was gone.

The subjeckies threw in a metal cage outside surrounded by tall trees. A chain connected them to branches, holding them in the air.

Rozel rocked the cage back and forth, hoping it would break but only shook the leaves off the branches. Xui just sat there. He was meditating. Rozel was annoyed with the lack of help he was getting. "Xui could you give me a hand?" he asked holding the metal bars.

"Sit down, Rozel," Xui responded. His eyes remained closed.

"Xui, we are stuck in a cage and our powers are gone. Why are you sitting there calmly?" Rozel said.

"Sit down and shut up," he demanded. "You will attract animals... I know why our powers are gone."

"How?!" Rozel shouted. He caught himself and held his mouth closed.

Rozel sat across from Xui and asked softly how they lost their abilities.

"From us being confined in the metal box. It restricted any energy from the elements. Because we were disconnected from our element for so long we lost the senses of finding it."

"Will we get them back?" Rozel asked.

"Yes, and you're going to be the reason why. Close your eyes and meditate," Xui instructed. Rozel began to do the steps Xui was suggesting. Xui told him to find any source of water around. Connect with it again. Once he did, Xui would turn the water into ice and strike the cage open.

Rozel tried hard to concentrate. But the heat was frustrating him. "It's so hot, the air is too dry."

"Don't lose focus. Learn from me, I'm use to the cold. But you don't hear me complaining." Xui remained steady.

Rozel broke his posture. "You have more patience than I do." His eyes looked at Xui. Rozel had got an idea. Rozel had noticed Xui sweating heavily. He knew it was a long shot, but tried to bend it. It was a liquid so it occurred to him that it may be possible. Rozel moved his hands back in forth. Similar to the motion of the ocean. Suddenly the sweat lifted off of Xui's forehead and neck, into the air.

"Concentrate, Rozel," Xui said cautiously.

"Um, Xui?" Rozel said trying to get his attention.

"Concentrate!" Xui said aggressively.

"But Xui?!" Rozel said excited looking the sweat.

Xui grew impatient. He opened his eyes and fixed his mouth to yell at him. "You need to focus! Stop distracting me and start meditating!"

"Reach your hands out." Rozel said smiling. He formed two droplets into a ball. "It's your sweat I got from you."

Xui's face lit up when he felt his sweat. He touched his face and it was dry. He stood up and began jogging in place.

"Wait what are you doing?" Rozel asked.

"This will make me sweat more. Try combining our sweat and make the ball bigger."

Rozel got up and ran into place. Once they had enough sweat, Xui asked Rozel for sweat and slammed it down on the floor.

"What are you doing?" Rozel screamed.

"Would you keep your voice down," Xui whispered harshly. He stepped on it. The puddle of sweat began to freeze. Rozel was upset. All that sweat was gone to waste.

"Ahh, I can see again." Xui said. He could sense Rozel's disdain. Xui told him to stand back and just watch.

Xui spread his feet apart. The ice glided with his feet. Xui could feel the cold liquid freeze over. Xui grabbed two of the bars from the cage and them. He broke them free.

Rozel was shocked.

They hopped down. The dirt on the gorund had been so hot from the sun.

The ice couldn't freeze against the heat. Xui needed something to protect his feet. He ripped his shirt up and tied the fabric around his feet and started running. Trying to find any other source of water.

★ ★ ★

Hours later, Xui and Rozel still hadn't found any source of water. Rozel guided him through the island.

Their mouths were dry and they were becoming dehydrated. They bodies no longer could produce sweat.

A siren went off in the distance. Xui heard people scream, "Find them!"

He told Rozel they had to take off and run.

Rozel was still holding onto Xui's hand.

They made it through most of the island, until Xui tripped and fell down a hill. Rozel tried to chase after him, but he was too late. Xui was already falling, collecting dirt and bugs on his way down.

"Are you okay?!" Rozel was still galloping down the hill. When he made it to him, he was trying to help pick him up.

Xui stood up on his own. He wiped off the bugs he felt on his chest. He was annoyed.

Rozel started to help dust him off. "Are you okay?" he kept asking. "I'm so sorry."

"You know, I never met a person who is blinder than I am."

Rozel laughed. "Then again you have been locked on a world for years, isolated from people."

Xui paused. "Thanks. I'll remember that when you fall down a hill. I'm going to say that I'm sorry, and maybe you fell because I've been so isolated I don't know how to help you'." Xui gently pushed Rozel and they started laughing.

"Plus, you're blind. So you can't see where I am going to end up anyway," Rozel added, laughing excessively.

"You just know how to ruin the mood," Xui said mushing his head back. Xui was starting to have love for Rozel, like a little brother.

Promptly after they walked back up the hill, Rozel spotted a dark cloud of smoke. It was coming from a factory that was up ahead. Xui said to be careful; he didn't know who they were up against.

Rozel's eagerness reflected. He wanted to make it to the factory quickly. Rozel was trying to help guide Xui. But the heat was becoming almost unbearable to walk in.

In their course, a smell lingered in the air. It was coming from the factory. The closer they walked, the more the smell grew. It was strong and gassy. They cover their mouths as they coughed.

They made it to the pathway that lead to the factory doors. Rozel was ready to explore it, but Xui told him that they shouldn't charge into the building, until it was safe.

They hid behind a tree and Xui started meditating. Rozel knew that he should too if they were going to find any source of water.

Behind the factory was a shore.

Rozel suggested that Xui wait while he goes and reaches the shore.

Xui agreed.

Rozel snuck off finding his way around the factory. He noticed that there was no protection around the perimeter.

At the shore, the water rushed through the golden sand.

Rozel slowly walked through the water, smiling from the refreshment. He started to feel the water flow through him. Shocking his body like electricity, as he moved his hands in the motion of the waves.

The water lifted up to his command. Rozel had regained his power.

In the sky, Rozel noticed something flying. At first he believed it to be girties, but they were much bigger than that. Rozel started waving his hands, thinking it may be someone who could save them.

As he jumped, he saw it grow larger, they definitely were not girties.

Fear struck Rozel as he started running away.

He was stopped and blocked by two giant phigons. It was Grastem and Myosin.

Rozel was relieved. He ran up to them hugging their feet, because their bodies were too big.

Shifting back, Grastem and Myosin reconnected with their little brother. Investigating him making sure he was okay. Rozel told them that Xui was waiting for him and that they needed to go back for him.

When they discreetly made it back to the tree where Xui was left, he was no longer there. Myosin asked if he could have gone into the factory but Rozel felt that because he was blind he couldn't have.

Suddenly he remembered that Xui has good hearing. During the time Rozel left, Xui had been meditating. Trying to sense out the place. He could hear voices inside the factory.

After a while, Xui sensed a strong power inside. With the urge to find his brother, anything was possible. He got up and followed his senses and began scouting out the factory, going straight through the front doors.

They decided to all enter the factory underground.

Grastem made a tunnel, Myosin used fire to light the way. They came across a metal barrier. She melted it and made it inside the factory.

Rozel suggested that they should split up to find Xui. He described him as a tall blind guy with immense power. Myosin said that Grastem should go with Rozel, just so Rozel couldn't get lost again. Myosin wanted to go alone. She wanted to face whatever mess she had to deal with.

Grastem and Rozel decided to let her go. They both went up the steel stairs, and Myosin stuck to the ground level.

CHAPTER 24

REUNITED

X UI WAS USING his hearing to make out his path. He bent down on the floor, and felt around it. It was cold. Water from the island was rushing below the factory, circulating the cold through the air.

He took off the fabric from the shirt wrapped on his feet, and placed his foot on the ground. Through the cracks in the ground, frost began to surround his feet, giving him his sight through the vibrations.

He cracked the ice and the soundwaves scouted out the factory. Through his eyes, he saw them at white lights guiding him where to go.

It took him to a part of the factory that had a closed volt.

Xui touched around the door trying to find something to break through. He covered a part of it with ice and slammed down with his fist, trying to find an opening with the vibration.

He found a crack in the door. He slid a sheet of ice through, then expanded it, breaking open the door.

In the room had been technology Xui had never seen. Wires connected computers to each other. A young man whom looked identical to Xui sat on a chair, in the center of the volt, unconscious. There were wires connecting from him to the computers using him like a battery.

Tubes were connected to his arms and legs, draining blood from his body.

There was a bag above his head that dripped a liquids in his body. It was causing him to sleep.

Xui sensed that it was no other than Zender the Electric Phigon. His long lost brother, whom he, at one point, believed was dead.

Xui rushed to him. "Zen!" he was grabbing and shaking him. "Zender wake up!" Xui was removing the tubes and wires attached to his body. "What is this place?"

Zender wasn't responding. He was moving like a ragdoll from Xui pushing him.

Rozel and Grastem noticed a trail of ice puddles. Following it, they saw Xui trying to pull Zender up.

"Xui!" Rozel said as he ran up to him.

He grabbed Zender's arm and helped lift him up, "Is this him? Your brother?"

"Yes?" He said confused, "Seriously are you blind too? We should look exactly alike."

"I can assure you he is not blind. He just loves asking obvious questions." explained Grastem.

"And you are?" Xui questioned.

"This is my brother, Grastem!" Rozel said eagerly.

"It's nice to meet you." Grastem reached his hand out. "I finally get to meet the man who is the new topic of discussion." Grastem snatched his hand back. He forgot that Xui couldn't see.

Xui's head was still but his eyes were wandering.

Rozel saw how Grastem was scoping Xui's eyes, "Uh," he laughed nervously, "Xui can't see you…" He looked at Xui. "He lost his sight to a witch."

"But there are no witches on Spascic," said Grastem.

"There was one," Xui mumbled. He was getting impatient. He lifted Zender with Rozel and tried to walk.

Xui depended on him to guide most of the way out.

They stood at the entrance. "Wrap your feet up, Xui." Rozel said.

They started to open the doors, which sounded an alarm. Workers from all angles came to surround them. They tried to bust through the doors, but they were stopped by five Phoenixes waiting for them outside.

"Rozel, fly them home. You will have to fly back east, around the volcano. Do not stop. Don't worry about me, I will be right behind you."

"What about, Myosin?" Rozel asked.

"Don't worry Rozel. We will be behind you. Go!" Grastem demanded.

Rozel shifted into his Phigon. Xui helped Zender get on Rozel's back.

Grastem shifted into his Phigon ready to battle.

The Phoenixes launched fireballs Rozel as he was flying away. Each fireball sounded like cannons. Grastem shielded them by creating a barrier made from the ground.

Two Phoenixes follow after him. Rozel dodged the fireballs. Rozel was maneuvering his way through their attacks. He was trying to lead them to the body of water that was up ahead.

Grastem was left to defend him against the other three.

Rozel was flying over the ocean. His best defense would be in the water.

He caused an indent in the ocean, diving right in. He surrounded them an air bubble so it was easy for Xui and Zender to breathe.

Rozel was still noticeable to the Phoenixes who continue to fire at him.

Xui had sensed them inside the water and created ice to cover the surface. But the fire from the Phoenixes broke through.

There powers were being matched.

Rozel sped up trying to lose them, but they were just as fast as he was.

Xui loosely shot balls of ice back at them. He couldn't see where he was aiming.

Rozel dove deeper to the darkest part of the water. He swam faster towards the east. The Phoenixes could no longer see.

Grastem was confident. But he knew it wouldn't be easy taking on three phoenixes.

As he was fighting, he noticed that their power was stronger than any other phoenix he had fought before. He felt he was taking on a three Myosins.

He was outmatched.

The phoenixes hit him with flames and took him down. He shifted back, and the guards continued to jump him while he laid on the ground, completely weak.

Grastem was dragged back inside the factory.

CHAPTER 25

THE CHANCE OF A LIFETIME

M YOSIN HAD BEEN wandering the halls of the factory. It seemed abandoned to her.

All the security was outside fighting Grastem.

While she wandered, she walked across what appeared to be a vent.

She crouched down closer and saw a staircase.

She lifted the vent, and gently set it next to her.

She walked down the stairs leading to a battle dome similar to the she trains in.

She saw in the distance a man sitting on a throne watching two men fight each other in combat. The man sitting was older looking and had a long white beard. But he looked healthy and very muscular.

Myosin approached the men fighting and began to clap because she was impressed with their technique.

Both men stop to look at her, then they charged at her. They began attacking with their fist cover in fire. But she dodged every hit that was thrown. Swiftly avoiding every swing and kick.

The man on the throne was amused. He leaned forward and concentrated on Myosin's technique. He could sense Myosin's power.

Soon after, Myosin stopped dodging and fired back with hits. Shooting flames from her hands with every blow.

The guy on the throne ordered them to stop.

The two men were trying to catch their breath.

Myosin was standing across from them checking her nails. "What were they doing... training? For what, ballet?"

Thhe old man stood up and told Myosin to approach him. "Sassy tongue you have there." The old man said.

"Stiff beard you have there." She said back.

"You have a lot of confidence for a young soul. What's your name?" he asked

Myosin put her hands on her hips, "Who's asking?" she said in a sassy tone.

The man stood, "Fire Emperor Wetchador. Prior king of Spascic and Ruler of The Golden Island."

"Wetchador?!" Myosin was shocked. She was not expecting to be running into Wetchador. "So you were the previous dictator." Myosin looked him up and down, crossing her arms, "Well I'm not impressed."

Wetchador was taken back, "Excuse me?" he demanded.

"Did you train them to fight like that? Like Fairies during their dance rituals." Myosin was trying to get to him.

"Watch your tone. Show respect in the presence of a King," said one of the subjeckies.

Myosin cleared her throat. "Previous king…" She said looking at him, "you were a king. You lost that title a long time ago."

Wetchador jumped down from his throne and stepped to Myosin. "Would you like to know how I became King?"

"You know," she said in a high sarcastic manor, "there are books for that. I came here to find my brother. I know you have him."

"As a matter of a fact, I do." Wetchador grinned. He snapped his fingers. Two guards came out dragging Grastem in big iron chains.

"Grastem!" she called out. "What did you do?"

"Three other hostages escaped because of this man. They were all valuable." He stated.

"Let him go," Myosin demanded.

Wetchador laughed villainously. "I will make you a deal young one. If you can defeat me in a battle, I will let him and you go free. Along with the others. No worries about anything."

"Well if you fight like twiddle Dee and twiddle Dum, I'm pretty sure this will be easy." Myosin prepared her stance.

"But… if I win. You will be forced to join my guild or your brother will be killed."

"Why not just kill him now?" she asked as she tossed her hand up at Grastem.

Wetchador lifted his hands up and smiled, "Because what's the fun in that?"

Grastem screamed desperately, "Don't do it, Mye! It's a trap!"

One of the guards punched him in the gut shutting him up.

"Is it a deal?" Wetchador asked.

"Why do you want me to join this guild?"

"I need someone strong and fierce like yourself to help me run things. You can help me train new recruits into becoming unstoppable soldiers. You will be a leader. Queen of this island if you will."

"You don't even know me. How do you know I want any of those things?"

"Because I can see the fire in your eyes. You are one of us. Black sheep of your society. Together we can dominate the world again as I once did."

Myosin looked at him with disgust. "Are we going to fight or not?"

Wetchador removed the cape he had worn revealing his shirtless muscular body. He had a necklace and a charmed potion bottle containing blood. He ripped it off and drank it.

Myosin sensed Wetchador's power growing larger, nearly reaching hers.

Wetchador attacked Myosin.

Myosin was trying to dodging but it was no good. Wetchador was quick and strong. He connected every punch. His fighting skills were incredible. Myosin was no match.

Myosin was defeated within minutes of battle.

Grastem tried calling out for Myosin, but was punched again in his stomach.

Wetchador laughed out loud, cheering himself on.

He looked down at Myosin trying to get up. "Are you done already? The fight just started." He taunted.

"Screw you," Myosin said. She spat at Wetchador's feet. "I will never join you."

Wetchador crouched down. "Now we had a deal. I always like to say 'Never say never' you don't know what awaits you." Wetchador got up. He stepped over Myosin and looked over at Grastem. "Tell you what. Now that you got a taste of what true power is, I will let you go..." He looked back at Myosin, "if you promise to reconsider joining my guild." He laughed at her, "I didn't even need to shift into my phoenix for this fight."

"Whose blood did you drink?"

Wetchador avoided the question. "I want you to think about it." He leaned in closer to Myosin and softly spoke to her. "Come back and represent us in the next Andromeda. With my fighting technique and your limitless power, I am sure you will be the victor."

Myosin didn't answer. He was too embarrassed from losing. Wetchador ordered the guards to help escort them back home.

CHAPTER 26

HOME AT LAST

ROZEL MADE BACK to his home safely. He took Zender to his room, where he could be treated.

He walked through the hallway, and saw his mother talking to Bernard. He ran into his mother's arms.

Ithilia's heart was no longer broken. The pieces that were once scattered, magnetized back into place.

Rozel tried to explain everything, but she hushed him. She wanted to live in the moment of her son being back home.

The subjeckies injected Grastem and Myosin with a liquid that healed all their wounds and injuries, before they flew away back to the Island.

Entering the doors to their home, they spotted Ithilia and Rozel hugging on the top floor. Myosin mumbled, "Thank the Gods" as he began to walk up the stairs.

"Rozel," Grastem said as he made his way up the steps.

Rozel released himself from Ithilia's grasp. "You guys made it back," he said relieved.

"You can't get rid of us that easy," Myosin jumped in.

"Where are Xui and Zender?" asked Grastem.

"They are getting help. Zender hasn't awoken yet. But with treatment he should awake soon," said Ithilia

"Once he awakes, we shall have a feast. For the reuniting of our family, and welcoming our new friends," declared Baggasin who came around the hall.

"The gang's all here." Grastem said.

"Not quite. Where is Salomne? Has he been aware of my absences?" Rozel asked

"He is training with Kueir in the Air Pyramids." Myosin replied.

Ithilia shook her head, saddened.

"Let's not get worked up about it. We have Rozel back and everything is fine now. Right?" said Baggasin.

"Zender should be awaking soon. Let us get ready for dinner," said Ithilia as she dramatically turned to walk away.

CHAPTER 27

A NEW LIFE

X UI SAT AT the end of a bed. The nurses came in and out of the room to medicate and heal him as much as they could. They told Xui, that Zender has been induced with toxins that paralyzed his body.

Zender endured so much that it caused his body to go into a state of shock.

Xui had moved to the floor, "Now we can do what we were meant to do," mumbled Xui.

He was meditating trying to find peace. Under him laid a sheet of ice.

Zender's eyes slowly opened. His fingers cringed onto the bed. Xui heard the sound and shot over to the bed. "Zender!" he cried out.

"Xui?" he could hardly speak. "It can't be."

"Zender, it's me. It's Xui." Xui had tears in his eyes.

"Xui," he said, smiling. "Am I hallucinating?"

"This is real, brother. This is real." His voice was cracking.

Zender attempted to lift up. It caused him to cough. When he cleared his throat he reached to feel Xui's face. He then realized that he was not imagining him.

"I'm here, Zen, it's me. It's been forever."

"Where did you go? Why did you leave me?"

"Leave you….? Zender, I didn't abandon you. I was abducted. We were separated," Xui pleaded.

"I thought you were dead…"

Zender looked away. "I thought I was a dead man at some point."

"Your blood was being drained from your body. Why? Who was doing this?" Xui asked.

Zender's mind was wandering. "You had been gone for so long. I lost hope."

"Zender!" yelled Xui trying to get his focus. "Who was doing this to you?"

He looked into Xui's eyes. He noticed Xui's eyes didn't stay in one place. They wandered the room searching for the sound waves. "Wetchador."

"Father?" Xui was confused. "Why?"

"He was using my blood to create an army of power Phoenixes. The island you rescued me from had been an abandoned island until Wetchador created a civilization. Rebels against phigons joined his guild. I wasn't only a prisoner, but I was a test subject. When Wetchador found out my blood increased his power for a limited time, he used me as a blood bag. And because our blood regenerates quickly, I produced a limitless supply of blood for him. He used it to create an army of super phoenixes.

With the blood of a Phigon and his fighting ability, he will be unstoppable. Him and his army," explained Zender.

"All those years you've been nothing but a source of power. I thought you were the lucky one. I always had a feeling that you were still alive. Call it twin's intuition..." He chuckled. "... I also lost hope as well. I was a prisoner to a world created just for me. But it was for false reasons. I lost my eyesight trying to escape. I guess we both were captives in different ways," said Xui.

"Who took you?" asked Zender.

"Myrtle Merlow. Spascic's first witch. She took me and tried to mold me as a replacement to her son. When I finally caught on... well look at me." He pointed to his eyes. "We never had a chance at life."

"I heard you," Zender said. "What did you mean we can do what we were meant to?" Xui looked up, confused.

"You weren't supposed to hear that." He replied.

"Xui, leave the past in the past. We can start a new life. Times have changed. It may be hard to adapt to but we can start over."

Xui starred in the distant. "I have had two things on my agenda. Getting you back and getting my rightful place as King."

"Your greed was the reason all this has happened to us." Zender blurted out.

"What's that supposed to mean?" Xui questioned.

"I didn't mean that," Zender said apologetically.

"Yes, you did. It's okay. I deserve it. Fighting father, showing my true power caused him to see us as a threat."

"Father's greed is his own demise. Even now he yearns for more power." Zender told Xui.

"How are you feeling," Xui said. He was trying to change the subject. "Rozel and his family are throwing us a feast for our welcome into their home. Do you feel up to it?"

"I'm fine. I would love to meet our rescuers," Zender said.

"Get ready then, bolt." Xui called him a nickname Zender hated when they were children.

"I thought we were going to leave our past in the past."

Xui laughed. He got up from the bed and walked out the room.

When Xui walked down the hall, he was attacked in the shadows. A person dressed in black fluttered over him and smacked him with fairy dust, puting him in a sleep. The person threw him over their shoulder and scurried off with him.

CHAPTER 28

THE BLACK SHEEP

A BELL RANG THROUGHOUT the castle, alerting everyone that it was time to make it into the dinner room.

There was a table that stretched across the room fitting twelve seats. A maroon and orange colored apron lay across it. Everyone made their way around the table.

Rozel noticed Zender walking into the room alone. He was saving a seat for Xui to sit next to him.

Everyone took their seat as the servers plated them.

Zender looked at everyone and attempted to introduce himself, but was cut off by Rozel.

"Has anyone seen Xui?" Rozel asked.

"He went for a walk!" Grastem shouted before anyone could reply. The room awkwardly grew silent. "I mean… he said he wasn't hungry and said he was going to for a walk around the town."

"Xui is known to do those things," Zender agreed.

"So, you're a Phigon, huh?" Myosin said. "What's your power?" she asked flirtatiously.

"I-uh, I control lightning." Zender answered hesitantly.

"Nice, another form of fire." She said.

Zender smiled.

"Please excuse Myosin's behavior," Ithilia chimed in. "My name is Ithilia, I am your half sister." She reached to shake his hand.

Zender shook back; he tried to look for a resemblance, "My sister… How?" he asked.

"I am awfully embarrassed to say." She giggled, "I was conceived during an affair my mother was having with Wetchador." She explained.

"It's not your fault." He assured her. "You should not feel embarrassed. I never knew I had a sister."

"My mother was shunned out for adultery. But since I was Wetchador's last child alive, I was chosen to lead the Volcanic Tribe."

Myosin held her mouth as if she was going to throw up. "I just hit on my uncle… I'm going to barf." She said.

Rozel started to laugh at her misery. "Thanks to Myosin, I was able to save you and your brother." He said.

"Yes, thanks to Myosin, you nearly got killed." Ithilia added.

"Give him some credit, Ithilia. Without him, Rozel wouldn't have saved these lost souls." Baggasins stated.

"Myosin has been getting Rozel in some trouble and she lied to me. She has had the Shakawa the whole time. She knew who they were." Ithilia added

"Well, Mother, I know you look at me as a monster. But it was Rozel's curiosity that led us to this predicament. Curiosity killed the girtie, you know." Myosin said.

"This foolishness will lead you nowhere." Said Ithilia.

"Oh, Mother, please. I will not allow you to blame me for Rozel's actions." Myosin fought back.

"Let us calm down. We have a guest." Baggasins jumped in.

Ithilia ignored Baggasins, "Because you felt the need to encourage Rozel's imagination, it almost led him to be killed." She said.

"Almost! Key word is almost." She said try to justify.

"That is what I am talking about. You are selfish. I will not have someone like that leading this nation." Ithilia said.

"Wait, Mother. Let's not make any irrational decisions." Grastem said trying to prevent any actions.

"No Grastem, let her say it." Myosin said.

"You will no longer be representing The Volcanic Tribe in the Andromeda." Ithilia commanded.

"What?!" Baggasins shouted.

Myosin began to clap as she got up from her seat. "Congratulations mother. You must feel sooo accomplished." She said.

"Get out of my sight." Ithilia demanded.

"Don't worry, Mother," Myosin said harshly. "I will do something better for you. I will get out of your life." Myosin stormed off.

"Ithilia, the battle is in three years. You have no time to find another leader to represent this nation." Baggasin said.

"I will do it..." said Zender.

"Are you sure?" Ithilia said.

144

"Absolutely. I may not be in the best shape right now, but I do have the power to keep up. I will be honored." He added.

"No worries, Baggasin. Meet our new leader." Ithilia announced.

"No offense to you Zender, but mother you have no idea what you've done," Grastem told Ithilia.

Grastem chased after Myosin, only to find that she was packing her things into a bag.

She gathered as many things should could.

Grastem knew exactly where she was headed. He tried to use his words to convince Myosin to stay. But nothing could get through to her. Myosin tuned his voice out. Her mind was set.

Ithilia helped fuel the passionate fire that burned in Myosin's eyes. She craved nothing but power at that point. Myosin was going to prove that the Andromeda was hers. She was going to be Queen. She felt there was no more hope for her relationship with Ithilia or anyone else. It was time for her to leave.

Grastem had no words left to say. He watched as Myosin set off towards the east. Where the Golden Island was located.

The sky grew amber as the sun was setting.

Myosin flew over to the golden island. She saw the factory where she previously had faced Wetchador. But noticed in the distance ahead, there was a tall building. It was skinny like a pillar. It was like a castle. Instead of flying back to the factory she headed to the building. At the tip of the building was a flag that flapped in the wind. Myosin flew down at the entrance of the building. Only to be welcomed by two men guarding the doors.

Two Phoenix gargoyles were set on the side of each end of the steps.

When she walked inside, and met with Wetchador.

He told Myosin to follow him up the spiral staircase.

They made it into a room filled with books. Wetchador announced that he knew Myosin would come back to him. He saw a lot of himself in Myosin. Myosin asked, why during their fight, he didn't use any fire. Wetchador laughed. He pulled his hand forward, and conjured a blue flame at the center of his palm.

Myosin was amazed. Wetchador offered to teach her Blue Fire, an ancient technique the phoenix ancestors used. It is forbidden technique but it will help her win the Andromeda.

Wetchador wanted to know how bad she wanted the throne. She was insulted that he would even ask that question.

She wanted to know how she would be able to participate in the battle. There were four slots and they all were being taken.

Wetchador told her that he created a new nation. The Golden Island. There had always been four nations. But now that there is a fifth, and so there can be a fifth contestant.

Wetchador asked for something in return. He wanted to feed from Myosin's blood. Every month he wanted Myosin to drain blood into a supply bag that will last him.

Myosin didn't hesitate to agree. She knew with the power Wetchador possessed, she could beat Salomne in the Andromeda. Although she was confused as to why Wetchador wanted her blood. Myosin didn't want to waste any more time. She wanted to start training so she could catch up to Salomne.

CHAPTER 29

FACE TO FACE
WITH DESTINY

X UI WOKE UP in chains. Celia was at the end of
the room crushing snake eyes in a small bowl.
She could hear Xui groaned himself awake. He tried to
yank away from the chains but there was no use.

The chains lifted him off the ground so he was
unable to use the vibrations to see his surroundings. He
was defenseless.

"Oh, great. You're awake now," Celia said.

"What is up with the people of this day and age,"
replied Xui. "Sneak attacking. Using metal as the first
resort. Why not fight me head on." He aggressively
yanked on the chain once more. "Cowardly if you ask me."

Celia put down the utensils she was using and stared at the wall in front of her. She was annoyed with his remarks. "What's wrong, afraid of a little metal?"Celia looked over at him and noticed him struggling to look around. But she didn't care. She went back to crushing the eyes, "…Said to be one of the greatest Phigons of all time, yet you are afraid."

"I wouldn't use that term. More so confused…" said Xui. "How do you know who I am? Was it you who captured me?" he asked.

"Xui, isn't it?" she asked. "I know you are blind. And unless you are touching the ground, you cannot see."

"You know something, you are really smart." He was being sarcastic, "You stated the obvious and that is I am blind. Good job mega mind. But anyone could've known that just by looking at my eyes."

Celia was growing more annoyed with him. She was trying to keep her composure, "I also know your true intentions here."

"Oh really? And what is that?" he asked

"Power. You plan on entering the Andromeda. You want the throne. And will do nothing to get it."

"And what made you think of this assumption?" Xui asked

"It's not an assumption. I know this of you. You planned all of this," she said. Celia grabbed the bowl she was using and poured the result of the snake eyes into a pot where there were other liquid ingredients. "I am going to make you tell me." She walked over to Xui and held the pot in his face. The smell coming from the pot was vulgar.

"Wow. So this was what you were doing. Shitting in something, just to hover it in my face." Xui antagonized.

Celia grabbed his face, squishing his lips harshly together. "This will make you speak the truth."

"If you think I am going to eat this garbage, you are highly mistaken." He said, snatching his face away.

"This will kill you if you eat it." She put the pot down. "As much as I would love for that to happen, I need you alive."

Celia dipped her hands in the warm pot; covering her hands in the concoction. She drew a symbol on Xui's forehead of a snowflake. Then put her hands on the sides of Xui's face.

"Get off of me," Xui growled. "Get this filth away from me!" He was pulling away and tugging the chains trying to escape.

"What's wrong, Xui? Something to hide?" Celia said.

Celia closed her eyes and a vision struck in her mind.

Xui snapped out of the chains. Breaking the stone wall he was chained to. His feet slammed on the ground, and ice spread the surface. It was giving him a glimpse of the room he was in.

Celia was scared and defenseless.

Xui saw Celia standing in front of him and pulled the chain to wrap around her and restrain her from moving. "Now how do you like it?"

"I knew it. I saw it, I saw you!" Celia said helplessly.

"You saw nothing," Xui growled at her.

Xui ripped the chains off his wrists and ankles. There was a fountain in the center of the room he heard. He walked over to it and froze it.

He walked up to Celia and removed the chains.

Xui clenched her neck and slammed her back into the broken wall. A piece of broken stone slice her back causing blood to fall.

Xui threw her to the ground and started looking around.

"Go ahead and kill me, you monster. You will be stopped."

Xui looked at her and laughed. "Kill you?" He continued to laugh. "I'm not going to kill you." He froze her feet, as she yelped from the chills she got. The ice covering her feet grew every few minutes. And if she tugged or tried and pull away, it grew quicker.

"This ice is my specialty. I learned this while I was trapped on the world one of you bitch witches kept me on. Now I am back to regain the throne. What you saw in that vision was me taking back what was rightfully mine." Xui's voice grew louder and more intense. "Stolen from me by the likes of you!"

Celia begged and cried for Xui not to do what he was going to do. But Xui already had his plan taken in action.

Xui crouched next to her. "This ice won't kill you, but it will freeze you until you are melted free by fire from another Phigon."

Xui stood up and walked out. He was setting out for power. Celia struggled to pull her feet from the ice but it made the ice grow to her knees. She was alone and out of luck.

Xui saw two guards standing outside. They didn't hear anything that had taken place inside the sanctuary. Xui made a sword of ice. He sliced off the heads of the guards, killing them instantly.

CHAPTER 30

STUCK IN A COLD SITUATION

SEVERAL HOURS HAVE passed since Xui left Celia.

The ice covering her has made its way up to Celia's neck. She was crying and praying that she would be set free. But it only made her time more difficult.

In the vision: *Xui had a crown being placed on his head. He was sitting in a chair made of vines and petals, laughing villainously. Xui was building an army. His soldiers had baby blue skin and bright white eyes. They looked like muscular snowmen. A war was about to break out. Water waves, blue fire, lightning bolts, and a gust of wind flashed in her head.*

She heard the Sanctuary door being opened. In stormed Salomne. He noticed her trapped and ran over to her questioning who caused this.

When he arrived to Fairold, the fairies made him of aware that Celia was still in the Sanctuary and had been there for hours. When Salomne made it to the entrance doors, he saw two guards decapitated. Their headless bodies had been lying in puddle of water. The sword Xui used to kill them had melted. Their heads were on the spears. Xui took from the guards, and he stuck in the ground.

Celia explained what was happening.

Salomne expressed his guilt for leaving, telling her he needed time to find himself. But he realized that Celia was going to be his queen when he won. That's what made him come back for her.

Celia was distraught. She told Salomne that being queen wasn't on her mind. She was afraid of what was to come.

"Salomne, I don't have much time left," Celia said as the ice continued to grow. "You need to know what you will be going against."

"Celia, is this the end?" he asked grabbing her face.

"I am not dying Salomne." she replied. "I need you to listen, there's not much time to explain. As upset as you are, I need you to let me go. This ice will keep me confined for some time. For now I want you to go back and train for the Andromeda." she said. "Xui is building an army. I don't what they are, but they will be monstrous."

"Everything is my fault. I should've known Grastem and Myosin couldn't handle this," Salomne said.

"This was fate, Salomne," she assured him. "I need you to forget about me and focus on your training." Celia was trying to comfort Salomne with her words. "Go back to the Air Pyramids and prepare for battle." The ice grew to her ears and began swallowing her face.

But just before it reached her lips she told him there was going to be a war. Salomne and siblings will each have an army. The war will take place once the new king is declared. Everyone will be against each other. The people he thinks are close to him will be the ones who turn on him.

The ice was covering her mouth. Her last words were "Trust No One."

CHAPTER 31

THE NEXT ANDROMEDA

ITHILIA'S TIME WITH her Rozel was up. She felt like she had just got him back and now he was leaving for three years to train. Though she knew this day would come, she was feeling guilty for not spending more time with him.

Rozel flew off to the Atlantic Nation. He was welcomed by all the people.

They were honored to be led by him. His power was a blessing to them.

Xui remembered Rozel was training for them and wanted to check in with him. Rozel was so excited to see him. He offered Xui a place to stay. In return, Xui would help train him.

Grastem had already set off to Fairold. That's where he belonged; most of his time was spent there. Grastem wasn't going to be able to see Hans as often as he wanted to. There was so much preparation he needed to do for the Andromeda. So Hans decided to move to Fairold to be closer to him.

Word got out that there was a fifth nation joining the fight. But no one found out who would be leading the nation in the Andromeda. Myosin liked the thought of keeping it under wraps. She wanted to throw the elemental of surprise at everyone.

Salomne headed back to the Air Pyramids.

He didn't stop at home to personally tell them about the vision. He felt that would take more time away from his training. Instead he wrote them letters.

In the letter it says:

> *Dear Family,*
>
> *I want to let every single one of you know how much I truly love you all.*
>
> *I am sorry for my absence in rescuing Rozel. For me to be the best brother and the best king, I needed to start my training. I trusted in Grastem and Myosin to rescue him, and they were successful. But I fear that was just the beginning.*
>
> *I am now reaching out for help. Celia is trapped. Xui has imprisoned her in ice. The ice cannot melt unless Myosin uses her fire, and sets Celia free.*

Just before she was attacked, she saw a vision of Xui. He is trying to take his place as king of Spascic. He also plans to start a war with each nation. All of us were fighting.

This is the first time I say her visions are wrong! I cannot see us fighting each other. Our bond as a family is too strong. As the oldest brother, I promise to prevent this war from happening. Now is the time to train and focus. Tap into your element. Let the spirits of the previous rulers guide you. We cannot let something else come tear our family apart again! I will win the Andromeda for us. I will rise to the throne and make sure that as a family, we stand together strong and loyal. I swear to the Gods. I will protect this family. Please join my cause, my loving family. Nothing will be able to stop us when we are together.

Love, Salomne.

Salomne kept it short and to the point. Xui's coming and he was coming for all of them.

When Grastem received the letter, he crumpled it up. He was disgusted that Salomne would rather write to them than see them in person. To him, all he saw in the letter was Salomne already declaring his victory in the Andromeda. He was a hypocrite. Nothing was more important to him besides that throne. Not even his family. Grastem swore he would win the battle just so Salomne couldn't.

Rozel received it and was appalled. He felt that Salomne didn't even give Xui a chance, yet Salomne judges him. Rozel didn't ask Xui about the letter. He kept it from him. He didn't believe in what the letter said. He knew Xui's heart, giving him the benefit of the doubt.

Salomne mailed off the letter to the Volcanic Tribe for Myosin. But instead it was Zender received it. Zender knew that Xui was going to be up to something. Although Xui is his twin brother, Zender wanted a new life. He didn't want Xui ruining what was going for him. Zender vowed to win the Andromeda for himself. With him in power, he hoped it would prevent Xui from doing anything that may cause them to be separated again. Permanently.

ABOUT THE AUTHOR

G ABRIEL SILVER. THIS author not only touches the hearts of this world, but the hearts of all galaxies. Already published as a poet with his poem, "The Colors of Emotions", Gabe Silver is ready to showcase his new novel, "The Phigon Chronicles", to the scene. Dealing with a fictional fantasy that reflects on the behaviors of everyday people. This series has been in his mind for over 10 years and has been writing it for over a year now, trying to perfect it. He hopes that his hard work shows through the Phigons. Readers get ready to put your glasses on. You will be taken into a whole new realm, with Gabe Silver's books.

Printed in the United States
By Bookmasters